SPECIAL MESSAGE TO READERS

THE ULVERSCROFT FOUNDATION
(registered UK charity number 264873)

was established in 1972 to provide funds for research, diagnosis and treatment of eye diseases. Examples of major projects funded by the Ulverscroft Foundation are:-

- The Children's Eye Unit at Moorfields Eye Hospital, London
- The Ulverscroft Children's Eye Unit at Great Ormond Street Hospital for Sick Children
- Funding research into eye diseases and treatment at the Department of Ophthalmology, University of Leicester
- The Ulverscroft Vision Research Group, Institute of Child Health
- Twin operating theatres at the Western Ophthalmic Hospital, London
- The Chair of Ophthalmology at the Royal Australian College of Ophthalmologists

You can help further the work of the Foundation by making a donation or leaving a legacy. Every contribution is gratefully received. If you would like to help support the Foundation or require further information, please contact:

THE ULVERSCROFT FOUNDATION
The Green, Bradgate Road, Anstey
Leicester LE7 7FU, England
Tel: (0116) 236 4325

website: www.foundation.ulverscroft.com

BABY ON LOAN

Jessie is temporarily caring for her adorable baby nephew when she gets evicted from her apartment! She has no choice but to let Patrick Dalton think she's a single mother, so that he'll let her stay with him. The last thing he wants is Jessie and her baby bringing chaos to his serene home — but in no time his life is filled with laughter and the very beautiful Jessie. Until he discovers that his growing love for his houseguests is based on a lie . . .

LIZ FIELDING

◆

BABY ON LOAN

Complete and *Unabridged*

LINFORD
Leicester

First published in North America in 2002

First Linford Edition
published 2016

A catalogue record for this book is available
from the British Library.

ISBN 978–1–4448–2695–1

Published by
F. A. Thorpe (Publishing)
Anstey, Leicestershire

Set by Words & Graphics Ltd.
Anstey, Leicestershire
Printed and bound in Great Britain by
T. J. International Ltd., Padstow, Cornwall

This book is printed on acid-free paper

Prologue

'It's awful. Like a mausoleum. You couldn't pay me to live there.'

'It's quiet. Jessie needs to be quiet to work.'

'No children, no pets, no music loud enough to escape through the walls. It's not natural.'

'Jessie doesn't like cats, is terrified of dogs and has no children.' Kevin didn't add 'lucky woman' because, although that was the way he felt right now, he was fairly sure that lack of sleep was warping his point of view.

'She never will have any children if she doesn't get out from behind that computer and get a life.'

'Is it compulsory?'

'Don't be flippant. Jessie thinks she's making the right decision but we can't let one rat of a man do this to her. And working from home doesn't help. At least if you go out to work you're forced to talk to people, interact with them, face-to-face . . . ' They exchanged a helpless look. 'You could die in the quiet of Taplow Towers and no one would ever notice.' The baby, who had been quiet for all of thirty seconds while he gathered breath, resumed his anguished protest against the imposition of teeth upon his tender little gums.

'No chance of that here.'

Faye ignored her husband, murmuring soothing noises of comfort to their infant son. It made no difference. He was suffering and he intended that the world should suffer with him. 'Did you see the look that woman in the lobby gave poor Bertie when we were leaving?' she continued, as if she hadn't been interrupted. 'As if he was contagious or something.' She paused to wipe the dribble from her darling's mouth. Then she said, 'I thought Jessie would be over Graeme by now. She was too calm about it, too controlled . . . She needs to let rip, get really angry — '

'Fall in love again?'

'Exactly! And the sooner the better. Cutting herself off like that isn't normal — '

'This isn't normal.' Giving up any hope of sleep, Kevin rolled out of bed, took his small son from his wife and couched him under his chin, with scarcely a break in the stride pattern that was beginning to wear a path in the carpet.

'He's teething. It won't last,' Faye assured him as she collapsed into bed.

'You said that last week.'

'We just need a good night's sleep.'

'A good night's sleep? What is that, exactly? I have this dim recollection — '

'Stop complaining and think while you walk. We've got to do something to help your sister. She's about to sign a five-year lease on that horrible place — '

'It's not horrible. It's a very nice apartment. Safe.'

'She's too young to want 'safe'. It won't be good for her, Kevin.'

He caught the reflection of himself as he passed a mirror. Dark shadows, grey complexion. 'This isn't good for me. I need to sleep. Not just for a night. For a week.' He turned to his wife; she didn't look any better. 'So do you.'

'Yes, I do. We do.' And then she smiled, drowsily. 'That's it, then. Problem solved.'

1

'Please, please, please, Patrick! Everyone's going. There won't be a soul left here in London — '

Patrick Dalton resisted, without much difficulty, the urge to smile. 'Just you and the other seven million — '

'Don't laugh at me! I'm being serious!'

Laugh? She had to be joking. He wasn't in the mood for laughing. Or indulging his niece. The way things were going, she'd be off the hook soon enough; meantime, it wouldn't hurt her to behave herself for once.

'So am I, Carenza.' The formal use of her name was usually sufficient warning that she was pushing her luck. 'You seriously promised to look after the house while I was away. And I seriously trusted you to keep your word or I would have used my usual house-sitting service.'

'I thought you said they couldn't find anyone at such short notice?'

She was so sharp it was a wonder she didn't cut herself with her own tongue. 'I believe I said it would be *difficult* for them to find anyone at such short notice.'

'Oh, don't be so . . . so . . . lawyerish!'

'Don't knock it, Carrie, it pays the bills. Quite frequently they have your name on them.'

Unabashed, she changed tack. 'You could call the house-sitters now and ask if they could find someone. Couldn't you?' Even the hollow echo from the communication satellite couldn't disguise the wheedling tone that was supposed to have him twisted around her little finger.

'Now? Correct me if I'm wrong but, whilst it's the middle of the day here, I'm pretty sure that it's the middle of the night in London. I don't think the agency — '

'Later, then,' she pushed, her keenness apparently undiminished by his obvious lack of enthusiasm. 'You could call the agency later.'

'I could,' he agreed tersely, 'but what would be the point?' A fraud case that he'd put weeks of work into and was scheduled to be in court for a minimum of three months was collapsing about his ears, which left him disinclined to submit to the wheedling of his eighteen-year-old niece. 'You haven't got the money to go gallivanting around Europe or you wouldn't be spending your summer in London house-sitting for me and, by the way, using my phone to call me long-distance.'

'It's the middle of night,' she reminded him. 'Cheap rate. And actually that was the other thing.'

'What was?'

'Money. I thought maybe you could lend me some until Mummy comes to her senses.'

'To go backpacking around Europe for the summer? Are you crazy? Your mother would have a fit.'

'I wouldn't tell her if you didn't.' She

gave a little-girl laugh that didn't fool him for one minute.

'Nice try, sweetheart, but forget it.' Europe was going to have to remain a dream for her this year. 'Get better grades when you do your resits in November and I'll give you a nice fat cheque so that you can go skiing at Christmas. Meantime, I suggest you use the long, friendless weeks ahead of you to revise, revise, revise.'

Carrie said something very rude about revision. 'How can you be so mean?'

'It takes practice, angel.' And he'd had a lot of practice. Some women refused to take a gentle hint. 'Tell me, how are my precious, er, *ficus*? You're not forgetting to spray them, I hope?' Her response, as he had anticipated, was brief and alliterative. 'Luke-warm water, don't forget,' he responded, mildly.

'Okay,' she said, with a sigh. 'I'll do it now. I'll spray them with luke-warm water and then I'll take them out of

their pots and cut off all their roots.'
And then she hung up.

Patrick laughed, feeling a great deal
better for the exchange. He certainly
wasn't worried about the wretched house
plants; they had been her mother's idea,
as was the complicated care routine that
she'd invented for them. His sister had
prevailed upon him to ask the child to
house-sit for him while he was in the
Far East. What Carenza needed, Leonora
had asserted firmly, was some responsibility, something to make her feel trusted,
something to keep her in London and
her mind on her resits. Against his better
judgement, he'd agreed.

And he'd had to have someone. He
couldn't leave the house empty for the
length of time he'd anticipated this case
would take. But two weeks of spraying
house plants had clearly taxed Carrie's
capacity for responsibility to the limit,
especially now her friends were desert-
ing her for the pleasures of Europe.

Tough.

Jessie turned off the shower. Someone was ringing her front-door bell and it appeared to be stuck. If it wasn't stuck, someone was going to need a very good reason for making such a racket.

'All right! I'm coming!' she called as she reached for her bathrobe, wound a towel around her dripping hair and headed for the door. As she drew back the bolt the clangour abruptly stopped, although by now it had probably woken up half the residents of Taplow Towers which would not make her Miss Popular at six-thirty in the morning.

She slipped on the chain, turned the dead-lock and opened the door a few inches. There was no one there. Then she looked down. Looking back up at her, with eyes that could melt ice, was Bertie.

She melted momentarily, then because Bertie, clever though her adorable nephew undoubtedly was, couldn't have rung the bell himself, she undid the chain.

10

'Faye? Kevin? What's wrong?' she asked, flinging back the door.

Her brother and sister-in-law were noticeable only by their absence. There was just a little yellow note in Kevin's handwriting, stuck to the gleaming woodwork. She peeled it off, held it up to her face and squinted at the words. Certain that she must have misread them, she fumbled for the spectacles in the pocket of her robe. The words leapt into bright focus. 'Please take care of Bertie for a few days,' she read. 'We'll explain when we get back. Love, Kevin and Faye.'

Get back? Get back from where? Something had to be wrong! Very wrong!

Three floors below she heard the lift door opening. 'Kevin!' She edged round Bertie's buggy and headed for the stairs. 'Wait!' She was halfway down the first flight of stairs when she was stopped by the disapproving voice of her neighbour from the floor below.

'Is something wrong, Miss Hayes?'

In Jessie's ordered world nothing was ever wrong. She anticipated practical problems and dealt with them before they could develop. And these days she was careful to avoid emotional ones.

A few feet above her Bertie snuffled in his buggy, gave a little whimper and, with a horrible sinking feeling, she acknowledged that she might have been getting complacent. Far below her, the front door banged shut. This was practical *and* emotional and she was in deep trouble.

Taplow Towers was a haven of peace and tranquillity. No loud music, no pets and definitely no children, apart from brief visits confined to the hours of daylight.

Dorothy Ashton, chairperson of the Residents' Association, with ears as finely tuned as those of a bat, glanced up as Bertie whimpered again, in what Jessie feared was a prelude to something much louder. 'What was that?' she demanded, suspiciously.

'Nothing.' Jessie cleared her throat,

loudly. 'I'm just a bit wheezy, that's all.' She gave a little cough to demonstrate. 'I'm sorry about the noise. I was in the shower and I couldn't get to the door in time.' But not by chance she was certain. The reason for the early-morning visit was to ensure that she'd being wearing nothing but a bathrobe and a frown and wouldn't be able to pursue her brother to demand an explanation.

And it had worked. Better than he could have hoped, because pursuit was now further hampered by the necessity of getting Bertie into her apartment without Dorothy Ashton seeing him.

She waved the note as evidence of her probity as she backed up the stairs. 'It was Kevin. My brother. He left a note.' Then, coughing again and clutching at her robe to discourage any inclination the woman might have to follow and press home her complaint, she said, 'Please excuse me, I think I left the shower running.' She smiled, apologetically.

Lady Ashton was not to be moved by a smile. 'You know we will not tolerate noise nuisance, Miss Hayes. You're still on a probationary tenancy. Your visitors on Sunday were very loud — '

'I know and I'm sorry, but Bertie's teething. I did take him out for a while.' She'd offered to take him for a walk to give her neighbours a break, holding his warm body close as she'd walked the path around the little park in the centre of the square. Kevin and Faye, poor loves, had both been asleep on the sofa when she'd got back. 'It won't happen again,' Jessie added, quickly. 'I promise.' Nothing . . . nothing was going to ruin her chances of staying at Taplow Towers.

It was peaceful. Quiet. Utterly predictable. Taplow Towers wasn't the kind of place where good-looking men knocked on the door when they ran out of coffee. She should have realised that someone who could flirt as skilfully as Graeme must have had a lot of practice. And, sooner or later, would run out of coffee again.

At Taplow Towers she could work all day, and all night when she wanted to, at her computer without the slightest risk of disturbance. She'd had all the disturbance she could take . . .

Not that it had been easy to get in. The Residents' Association felt safer with ladies of 'a certain age' but her somewhat disingenuous statement that she had 'lost' her fiancé had been received with a tactful change of subject and, apparently reassured that her heart was broken beyond mending, she'd been given a probationary tenancy. It still had a month to run. One false move and she'd have twenty-four hours to vacate the premises. It was in the rules and she'd signed on the dotted line without a qualm.

A little grovelling might be wise, she decided. 'I'm truly sorry to have disturbed you, Lady Ashton.'

'Very well, Miss Hayes. We'll say no more. This time.' And she finally smiled. 'Everyone is allowed one mistake.' Behind her the snufflings were getting louder and Jessie's cough took on epidemic proportions as she continued to back up the stairs. 'You should take some honey and lemon for that cough, dear.'

'Yes.' Cough, cough. 'I will.' Cough. 'Thank you.'

The moment that Dorothy Ashton retreated into her own apartment Jessie turned, grabbed the handles of Bertie's buggy and wheeled him inside, shutting the door very quietly behind her.

Then she turned and leaned against it, pulling the towel from her hair, swamped by warring feelings of exasperation and longing as she looked down at her infant nephew.

His little face was screwed up into a man-sized frown as he tried to focus on her and, in an attempt to reassure him, she leaned closer. 'Well, Bertie,' she murmured as she stroked his downy cheek with the back of her finger. 'This is a fine mess you've gotten me into.'

It was a mistake. Jessie's height and colouring was similar to Faye's, but Bertie knew his mother's voice. This wasn't his mother. He opened his mouth, determined to let not just Jessie but the entire world know exactly how he felt about that.

'Shh!' she said. 'Shh! Please, Bertie!' Jessie knew very little about babies, but enough to understand that if she couldn't keep him happy, and quiet, her days at Taplow Towers were numbered. She picked him up, put him to her shoulder. 'I'll find your mummy and daddy . . . soon. It'll be fine. I promise.' Bertie, for some reason, wasn't convinced.

Instinctively she began to walk back and forth across the thick, sound-deadening carpet, the way that Faye had done on Sunday. She had a momentary recollection of her sister-in-law's pale and exhausted face. Kevin hadn't looked much better and he had to go to work . . .

And now some other nightmare must have befallen them. As she passed her desk, she grabbed her phone. She doubted that Kevin and Faye would be at home taking calls, but she could leave a message. They'd check for messages, surely? No matter what emergency had called them away?

But she didn't have to leave a message. They had left one for her.

'Jessie, darling, we need sleep, I mean *really* need sleep, and Faye thought — we thought — since you're not just Bertie's aunt but his godmother, you wouldn't mind — '

Faye interrupted him. 'There just wasn't anyone else we could ask — '

Ask? Ask? They hadn't asked, because they'd known what the answer would be! They knew she couldn't have a baby at Taplow Towers!

'I'm taking Faye away for a few days, no phones, no babies,' her brother concluded. Then, as an after-thought, he added, 'We'll do the same for you one day. Promise.'

'Fat chance,' she snorted. Then, horrified by the enormity of her problems, she stared at Bertie. Bertie stared back for a moment before gathering himself to let rip. 'No, Bertie!' she begged. 'Please, darling!' Bertie wasn't listening.

Everyone else was.

* * *

'This is the final call for the British Airways flight to London, calling at . . . '

Patrick took his boarding cards from the check-in clerk and headed for Departure. It was Carrie's lucky day. Thanks to his client changing his plea — he'd almost certainly been paid handsomely to do so to protect people in high places — he was going home. Since there wasn't any chance of him sharing his house with anyone, let alone an eighteen-year-old girl, he would 'lend' her the money to join her friends in France in return for some serious promises regarding work. In twenty-four hours she would be free.

* * *

'So? Will you take it?'

Take it? Jessie had one hour before she was, to all intents and purposes, homeless. She would have been grateful for anything with hot and cold running water and a roof that didn't leak; this was beyond her wildest dreams. More importantly, it was available immediately. Now. This very minute. It seemed almost too good to be true.

'I can move in right away?' She needed to reassure herself that she wasn't simply hallucinating. Twenty-nine hours without more than twenty minutes of consecutive sleep and absolutely no peace of mind could do that to you.

'Absolutely!' Carenza Finch seemed rather young to be a householder on this scale but Jessie was beyond worrying about it. 'I can't leave the house empty, and besides, I've got to have someone I can trust to feed my darling Mao while I'm away.' The cat, the one fly in the perfection of the arrangement, blinked at Bertie, who was perched on Jessie's hip. Bertie stopped grinding his gums into her shirt and stared back. 'I was at my wits' end.'

'Really?' *Was there an epidemic? Could you get immunised? Was she losing her mind?*

'Absolutely. So if you're happy, I just need the rent,' she prompted, 'and the place is yours, lock, stock and whatsit for three months.' She held out a pen. 'All you have to do is sign on the dotted line.'

Jessie fished her spectacles out of her pocket and, propping them on her nose, glanced at the lease with eyes gritty from lack of sleep. It appeared to be a standard form used by the agency she'd contacted. She signed it quickly and counted out the deposit and three months' rent in advance. In cash. Neither of them had time to wait for a cheque to clear.

Carenza Finch countersigned with a flourish, then she handed over the keys. 'It's all yours,' she said, as she gathered up the money and stowed it carefully in a money belt concealed beneath her sweatshirt. 'You will take really good care of Mao, won't you? He likes liver and fresh cod — you have to break it up with your fingers in case of bones — and minced chicken. I wrote it all down for you ... ' Jessie made a determined effort not to shudder. For a roof over her head, she'd mince chicken. 'Oh, and the drill for looking after the plants is on the notice-board.'

Oh, great. She'd try not to kill them, although anything tender was inclined to wilt if she went within ten feet of it. But she took her responsibilities seriously. Why else would Kevin and Faye leave their firstborn on her doorstep? They knew they could trust her.

Maybe she should do something utterly disgraceful in the very near future, something bad enough to give them second thoughts about doing this ever again.

'Have you left the vet's telephone number?' she demanded, following Carenza to the door. It wasn't that easy to be irresponsible. She was going to have to work up to it. 'And who do I call in the event of an emergency? Have you left your contact address?'

'I don't plan on having one for the

next three months,' Carrie said, picking up a heavy rucksack. 'Don't worry, nothing disastrous is going to happen.' Wrong. It already had. 'See you in three months.'

Three months. Breathing space to find another Taplow Towers. Not so bad. This thing with Bertie was just a temporary situation, after all. Faye was a doting mother; Kevin loved his son to distraction. Even exhausted, they wouldn't be able to live for more than a few days without him. And they must both know what this was doing to her life.

They would return, shame-faced and horrified at the ramifications of their actions; things would return to normal and within hours her life would be back on an even keel, running like clock-work. The only thing that wouldn't be the same was Taplow Towers.

If they'd just phoned, explained, she could have moved into their home for a day or two. Instead they'd shipped all Bertie's belongings to her by express carrier, along with a special delivery of disposable nappies. She knew what the parcel contained, because it was printed in large letters, all over the packaging. The porter hadn't said a word when he'd brought it up. He hadn't needed to. His mournful expression had been enough. She was doomed.

Lack of sleep must have been fugging their brains, because if it had been their intention to get her evicted, Faye and Kevin couldn't have made a better job of it.

None of which was Bertie's fault. She took a deep breath and dropped a kiss on his dark curls. Gave him a cuddle. She wasn't sure what it did for Bertie, but it made her feel a lot better.

'Sorry, sweetheart, but I'm going to have to put you down while I make a cup of tea.' Bertie, his big round eyes still fixed on the cat, went into his buggy without complaint. The cat yawned. Bertie wriggled delightedly and smiled.

Momentarily astonished by this phenomenon, Jessie paused and, for a heart-aching moment, she realised that her baby nephew was the most beautiful thing she had ever seen.

Damn Graeme.

The cat, meowing to be let out, distracted her from the yawning pit of self-pity. Bertie watched him as he sauntered down the garden, then whimpered as he disappeared into some bushes. Then howled.

'Oh . . . ' She glanced at Bertie and bit back the word that sprang to her lips. 'Mao!' she called. But he'd gone. Suppose he never came back? Two hours ago she wouldn't have cared, but if Bertie liked him she would buy free-range chicken from Fortnum's and mince it to paste for the precious creature. Maybe there was a picture of a cat somewhere . . .

★   ★   ★

Carenza picked up a discarded newspaper, using it to shade her eyes from the glare off the sea.

'Isn't that your uncle's case?' Sarah

said, turning her head upside down to read the headline. ' 'FAR EAST FRAUD TRIAL.' Yes, look, there's a picture of him.' She snatched the paper and grinned. 'Wow, but he's sexy!'

'Oh, puh-lease! He's old enough to be your father.'

'Only just.' She sighed. 'I remember him coming to speech day, years ago . . . He looked so lost. So . . . solitary. I fantasised for weeks about him. Comforting him, bringing him back to life . . . ' She pulled a face. 'Well, you know . . . '

Carenza rolled her eyes heavenward. 'I know. You and half the women in London according to my mother, silly cows. He'd lost the love of his life and his baby daughter. Getting over that kind of thing . . . well, I don't suppose you ever do. It's only work that keeps him going. Mum says if he doesn't ease off he'll probably end up Lord Chief Justice.'

'What a waste.' Then Sarah read, ' 'Defendant Changes Plea'? What does that mean?'

Carenza frowned, retrieved the paper from her friend so that she could see for herself, then groaned. 'What it means, Sarah, is that I'm in big trouble. I've let his house to a woman with a howling infant . . . ' They exchanged a horrified glance. 'And he's probably on his way home right now. How on earth could I have been so stupid?'

'You've had a lot of practice?' her friend offered, helpfully.

★ ★ ★

There were plenty of pictures. A Dutch still-life over the mantle in the semi-basement dining room next to the kitchen. A series of cartoons of barristers in wig and gown on the stairs, and a Stubbs upstairs in the drawing room. 'Look at the lovely horse, Bertie,' she prompted. Bertie was not impressed.

There were prints of famous nineteenth-century cricketers lining the main staircase and landing; she assumed they were famous, or no one would have bothered to frame them.

No cats.

The large bedroom was richly decorated in a warm red, furnished in antique walnut. It didn't quite go with Carrie's image; the cargo pants, the stud in her nose and the radical hairdo.

The second bedroom was furnished as a study, with floor-to-ceiling shelves containing law books. She remembered the cartoons and wondered if it was a family thing. Maybe her new landlady had inherited the house and the books. It would explain a lot.

There was a wonderfully large desk with room for her scanner as well as the computer. She hadn't had time to connect them, yet. Once Bertie was in bed, she promised herself, she'd make a start, try to catch up.

She hadn't been in the third room. Carrie had whizzed past, muttering something about it being a store room, not used in years. The door was stiff, as if it hadn't been opened in a while, but beneath the dust the room was painted in cheerful yellow and white so that it would look sunny on even the greyest of days. There were no pictures, though, just some boxes that looked as if they hadn't been disturbed for years.

She returned to the kitchen in the hope that Mao might have come back. He hadn't, but Bertie, overcome with exhaustion, finally dozed off in the crook of her arm.

Hungry, but anxious not to disturb the sleeping baby, she found half a packet of chocolate biscuits left by Carenza, settled carefully into a large and very comfortable armchair and tucked in to them.

She must have fallen asleep mid-bite because when Mao, miaowing and clattering his claws against the window, woke her, there were crumbs adhering to the chocolate liberally smeared down the front of her shirt; the remains of the biscuit had succumbed to gravity and were lying, chocolate-side-down on the carpet.

She let in the cat, bathed and fed Bertie and finally put him into his cot. Then she flung her crumby, chocolate-stained shirt into the laundry basket along with everything else she was wearing, pulled on a T-shirt because it was the first thing that came to hand, brushed her teeth and fell into bed.

In that brief moment before sleep claimed her, she had a momentary vision of the chocolate biscuit lying on the Persian rug in the drawing room and knew she should get up and do something about it.

And turn on the burglar alarm.

Then nothing.

* * *

Patrick dropped his bag in the hall and crossed to the alarm to punch in the code number. It wasn't switched on. Carenza had obviously forgotten to set it. He really should have known better than to give in to his sister's pleading and let her stay here.

Tomorrow he'd write her a cheque, she'd disappear like snow in August and everything would be back to normal.

Well, very nearly normal. It might be

the middle of the night in London, but he'd slept on the plane and it would probably take days for his body clock to readjust. Right now, he was wide awake and hungry.

He just hoped there was something edible in the fridge. He snapped on the kitchen light, swallowed hard and determinedly ignored the sinkful of unwashed dishes.

It was harder to ignore a faint, disturbingly familiar scent that he couldn't quite place. Probably because it was overlain with the smell of steamed fish.

The gritty crunch of biscuit crumbs beneath his feet distracted him, doing nothing to improve his temper. Forget a cheque. Carenza would be grateful to escape when he'd finished with her. House-sitting indeed. She couldn't be relied upon to sit in a cardboard box.

★   ★   ★

Jessie's first thought, as she woke up with a guilty start, was panic. It was too

31

quiet. She leapt out of bed, peered anxiously into the cot, then groped for her spectacles and put them on for a closer look. Just to be on the safe side. A week of this and she'd be a nervous wreck.

But there was nothing the matter with Bertie. In the faint spillage of light from the landing, she could see that he was fast asleep. She touched his cheek; it was warm, but not too warm. He was just fine. Gorgeous in fact, with a peachy bloom to his cheek and his dark hair curling softly around his ears.

The cat was fine, too.

She froze, horror struck. Faye would have a hissy fit if she could see her precious infant sharing his sleeping quarters with Mao, who had curled up and made himself thoroughly at home at the bottom of the cot.

She picked him up. He protested. Bertie stirred. She forced herself to cuddle the cat, murmur sweet nothings as she stroked him, even as her skin goosed at the touch of his fur.

Mao looked at her through suspicious, narrowed eyes as if he knew exactly what she was thinking as she tiptoed towards the door.

She had just made it to the landing when she realised what had woken her. There was someone in the kitchen.

2

Jessie had any number of choices. Call the police. Scream. Barricade herself in with Bertie and Mao and wait until the burglar had helped himself to whatever he fancied and went away. Scream. Confront the villain. Scream . . .

Oh, stop it! she told her wittering brain. The police. She had a mobile; she'd call the police. She pushed her spectacles down her nose and looked around. Where was it? When had she last used it? Oh, hell, it was in her handbag and that was downstairs. With the burglar. Which dealt with option number one.

And she'd thought her life couldn't get any worse.

Screaming, seriously screaming, and giving vent to all the anguish of the last two days had its attractions.

But screaming would wake Bertie

and frighten Mao and maybe the burglar wouldn't run away. Maybe he'd come looking for her in order to shut her up. Which thought was sufficient to put a hold on screaming. For the moment.

It would have to be option number three, then. The barricade.

She put the cat down and looked around. Memory and the light spilling in from the landing suggested that the furniture was of the kind that required a minimum of three heavily muscled men to shift. With a fourth directing operations. Except for Bertie's light-weight travelling cot, of course. Apart from the fact that it wouldn't stop a determined flea, Bertie was in it. Asleep. And no one was going to wake up Bertie if she could help it.

But any burglar worth his salt would certainly come upstairs looking for jewellery and money.

It was time for option four. No! Not screaming! And maybe not confronting the villain; she preferred to remain defensive if at all possible. What she needed, then, was something with which to defend herself. And Bertie. And, since he was her responsibility too, Mao.

She swallowed. And if there was more than one of them?

Refusing to think about it, she opened the wardrobe door and peered into the dark interior, desperate for inspiration. She'd been too busy to unpack and now she discovered it was full of dark, heavy clothes. Really, Carrie might have emptied the wardrobe of her gothic junk before she let the place . . .

She didn't have time to worry about it. What she needed right now was a sharply pointed umbrella, or . . . Something hard and heavy fell out and landed painfully on her toes. She bit back a yell of pain and bent to pick up the object.

It was a cricket bat. Brilliant. Odd — she didn't quite see Carenza leading out the England ladies' cricket team — but brilliant. She seized it and immediately felt more in control. Hefting it defensively in her hand, she crossed to the door, opened it a little wider in order to listen.

Before she could stop him, Mao shot through the gap.

★ ★ ★

Patrick opened the fridge. On the shelf inside the door, there was an open carton of milk; he sniffed it cautiously. It was fresh. He replaced it and explored further.

He took out a dish, uncovered it. It appeared to be mashed up fish. Unimpressed by Carenza's culinary skills, he rejected it, but as he opened a box of eggs something soft and warm brushed against his ankles.

Unnerved, he stepped back. The creature let out a banshee wail as he stepped on its tail, before tangling itself between his legs as it tried to escape.

Off balance and uncertain where he could safely put his feet, Patrick made a grab for the first thing that came to hand.

It was the shelf inside the fridge door.

It took his weight for a tantalising millisecond during which he thought he'd got away with it. Then, as shelf and door parted company, milk and moulded plastic succumbed to gravity and hit the floor. Patrick and the eggs were delayed slightly, while his head bounced off the edge of the work surface.

★　★　★

Jessie, dithering behind the bedroom door and wondering whether in fact the bat was such a good idea after all — she might just be handing the burglar a weapon — heard Mao's howl of outrage, swiftly followed by a horrendous crash.

Had the burglar killed the cat? Had the cat killed the burglar? Whatever was going on, it was clear that she could no longer hide upstairs. With the cricket bat raised shakily before her, she advanced slowly down the stairs and approached the kitchen with caution.

She'd been too tired to bother with clearing up before she'd fallen into bed, but, even so, the scene that met her gaze was a shock. Smashed eggs, milk spreading to form a small lake, a lake at which a perfectly content Mao was busy lapping, and in the middle of it all, flat on his back, blood oozing from a wound on his forehead, lay a man who seemed to fill all the available space. A man dressed from head to toe in burglar-black. Black chinos, a black shirt, sleeves rolled back to reveal thickly muscled fore-arms.

He was tall and strong and he would have disarmed her without raising a sweat.

Fortunately, he was unconscious.

Or maybe not. Even as she stood there, congratulating herself on the fact, he groaned and opened his eyes. Jessie grasped the bat tightly, swallowed nervously and croaked, 'Don't move!'

Patrick stared up at the ceiling. The kitchen ceiling. He was lying on the kitchen floor, in a very cold puddle, and his head felt as if it was about to fall off. And there was a wild-haired, semi-naked woman wearing spectacles two sizes too big for her, threatening him with his own cricket bat. Had she hit him with it? He began to raise his hand to his head in order to assess the damage.

'Don't move!' she repeated.

The words, undoubtedly meant to be threatening — although the effect was considerably diminished by the nervous wobble in her voice — were unnecessary. He had no desire to move. He just wanted to close his eyes and hope that when he opened them again all this would have gone away.

He tried it.

★ ★ ★

His eyes closed again. Jessie ventured a step nearer. He looked horribly pale and the gash on his forehead looked nasty. Oh, good grief, he was going to die. He was going to die and she'd get the blame and go to jail. That was the way it was. You read about it in the papers all the time. Burglar breaks in, burglar dies, innocent householder goes to jail.

Kevin and Faye would be sorry then . . .

She gasped. What on earth was she thinking of? He might have broken in, but the man clearly needed her help. She dropped the bat and paddled barefoot through the lake of cold milk to his side.

Stretched out on the kitchen floor he seemed very large, very threatening. Even unconscious he looked very dangerous. But she couldn't just leave him there. Grabbing a clean bib from the work surface, she knelt beside him and dabbed, tentatively, at the blood oozing from the wound on his forehead, forgetting her fear in her concern.

His eyes opened with an immediacy that suggested he hadn't been as far out of it as she'd thought, and he grabbed at her wrist. 'Who the devil are you?' he demanded.

'Jessie,' she replied instantly, not wanting to irritate him in any way. 'My name's Jessie. How do you feel?' She put real warmth into her voice. She really wanted him to know that she wasn't going to do anything bad . . .

'How do I look?' he countered.

He certainly didn't look good. Apart from the pallor, made worse by the dark shadow of a day-old beard, there was the blood which still hadn't stopped oozing. She put her fingers against his throat to check his pulse. It seemed the right thing to do, although she wasn't sure why because she could see for herself that he wasn't dead.

His skin was warm and smooth beneath her fingers, his pulse reassuringly strong. 'Well?' he asked after a moment. 'Will I live?'

'I th-th-think so.'

'I'd be happier if you could sound a little more convincing.'

He didn't *sound* like a burglar. But then, what did she know? 'Well . . . ' she began. Then something about the sardonic twist of his mouth alerted her to the fact that he wasn't being entirely serious.

'I won't struggle if you think I need the kiss of life,' he said, confirming her worst suspicions.

For a moment she was tempted. He might have broken in, but if he'd been the man in black leaving a box of chocolates she had the feeling any woman would be left wearing a smile. Maybe she should offer to kiss him better . . .

No! For heaven's sake, would she never learn?

And if he was well enough to joke, he was probably capable of getting up and . . . and maybe it would be better not to think about what he was capable of doing. Actually, she realised, as her brain stopped freewheeling and finally clicked into gear, she should stop wasting time and call the police and an ambulance. Right now.

'What you need is a trip to the nearest A and E department,' she said, primly, making a tentative attempt to free herself. He might be in a jokey mood, but she wasn't prepared to risk annoying him. His fingers remained clamped about her wrist as he tried to sit up. The effort was clearly too much for him and he subsided, with a groan, releasing her as he put his hand to his head.

Her mobile. She needed her mobile. Her bag was on the work surface next to the fridge and she stood up to reach for it. That was when her burglar grabbed her ankle.

And that was when she finally stopped being controlled and sensible and did what she'd been wanting to ever since she'd realised she had an intruder. She opened her mouth and screamed blue murder.

Patrick, who had simply wanted to know what this Jessie woman was doing in his house and where Carenza had disappeared to, decided that, after all, it didn't matter that much. Stopping her from screaming was far more important, so he tugged on her foot. Hard. The noise stopped abruptly.

Then she fell on top of him.

He muttered one brief word as the breath was knocked from him. One word was all it took to sum up his feelings. Her eyes, inches from his own, widened in shock, but before she could do or say another thing he grabbed her. 'Don't. Please don't say another word. I don't know who you are, or what you're doing here, but I give up. You win.'

'Win? *Win?*' Even to her own ears she was beginning to sound hysterical. Well, that was fine. She had every right to be hysterical. She was lying crushed against the chest of a ruthless criminal. A man who'd broken into her home. Who, even with a nasty head wound, was more than capable of taking advantage of the situation. And the situation was that while she was wearing a mercifully long and baggy T-shirt, there was little else to cover her embarrassment. Well, actually nothing else. All he had to do was move his hand a few inches and he'd discover that for himself.

She firmly resisted her brain's urgent prompting to tug her T-shirt down as far as it would go. That would only draw attention to her plight. Instead she forced herself to look him squarely in the face and tell him to let her go. Right now.

It was an interesting face. The kind of face that, under different circumstances, she'd like to see more of. On the thin side, but with strong bones, a lot of character, and she had the strong impression that pain was not a stranger to him. Yet his mouth promised passion. Oh, good grief. And she'd thought *he* was rambling!

'In what way, exactly, do I win?' she demanded, trying to get a grip of herself, gather her wits.

'I surrender,' he said. Surrender? What was he talking about? She stared at him. He had the most extraordinary eyes, she thought. Grey, but with tiny flecks of gold that seemed to be heating them up. Or was that just her imagination? 'Just don't scream any more. Please.'

'Do you mean that?' she demanded as fiercely as she could, not entirely trusting him. The wobble in her voice wouldn't scare a mouse.

'Oh, forget it. Give me a knife and I'll cut my own throat. It'll be quicker than the punishment you're dishing out.'

'Me!' she squeaked. 'I didn't ask you to break in and fall over.'

'Fall over?' he shouted, then winced. 'Is that going to be your story?' And he flung the arm that was holding her towards the cricket bat and grasped the handle. 'Haven't you forgotten exhibit A?' he said as he brandished it at her.

She scrambled to her feet and put some distance between them before he decided to beat her senseless with it. 'Just stay there,' she said. 'Don't you move. I'm going to call an ambulance.' She backed hurriedly away, ignoring the milk dripping from her T-shirt and running down her legs.

He dropped the bat. 'You'll have to drag me out into the street if you want it to run me over,' he warned her blackly.

Rambling. Definitely rambling. He needed to be in hospital, and quickly, but she moved well out of reach before she extracted her cellphone from her bag, dialled the emergency services and asked for an ambulance. They wanted details. 'I'm sorry, I don't know who he is. He broke into my house and he's fallen in the kitchen . . . '

'It's not your house!' he yelled. 'It's mine!'

'Head injury?' she repeated distract-edly as the ambulance dispatcher probed for details. Had he been watching the house? Had he seen Carenza leave and thought it was empty? He was regarding her angrily, but he hadn't moved an inch. Unconvinced by this evidence of co-operation, she stepped further back into the hall, leaving a milky footprint on the carpet. More mess. More bother. 'Oh, yes, he gashed his forehead on the corner of the kitchen unit . . . Yes, he's conscious, but he seems to be a bit odd . . . not quite making sense . . . I thought maybe he was, you know, on something . . . ' He groaned. She ignored him. 'Would you? And you'll inform the police. Thank you so much.' She hung up and returned to the kitchen, standing in the doorway, unwilling to get any nearer. One close encounter had been quite enough. 'They'll be here soon.'

'Tell me,' he asked, finally managing to heave himself into a sitting position and propping himself up against a cupboard, 'are you mad, or is it me?' He sounded quite serious, as if he really wanted to know.

Unwilling to say anything that might agitate him further, Jessie kept her distance, although her knees were shaking so much that if she didn't sit down soon, she'd probably collapse in a heap right where she was. 'Just keep still. I'm sure they'll be here soon,' she said, with a lot more calm conviction than she felt.

'Are you? I hope you're right. Tell me, where did that cat come from?'

Mao, having enjoyed the free spillage of milk and toyed with the yolk of one of the eggs, was now carefully washing his face. Jessie watched him for a moment. There was something almost hypnotic about the delicate, repetitive movements . . . 'I don't know. He belongs to the owner of the house.' She turned to him. 'It's one of the reasons she was desperate for someone to move in. She needed someone to look after him. It must have been a bit of shock to discover the house wasn't empty after all.'

'You could say that. Especially since this is my house.'

He was worse than she thought. Much worse. Jessie glanced at her watch, wondering how long it would take the ambulance to arrive. 'This is your house, is it?' she asked in what sounded, even to her own ears, a patronising attempt to humour him.

'Yes, madam, it is,' he said, sharply. 'And you can believe me when I tell you that I hate cats. And so does my dog. So maybe you'd like to explain what you're doing here?' Dog? He had a dog? She glanced around nervously. That was all she needed, a burglar who modelled himself on that Dickensian prototype Bill Sykes. But there was no slavering bull-terrier waiting to tear her limb from limb and Jessie, praying fervently for the early arrival of someone to remove this madman from her home, decided that humouring him would be the safest course.

'I'd love to — '

'Why don't you start by telling me — ?'

Upstairs, Bertie began to cry. She could have kissed him. Would kiss him. Right now. 'I'd love to stop and chat but I have to see to the baby.'

'Baby?' He looked, she thought, as if he'd been struck a second blow. 'You've got a baby? Here?'

'He's teething, poor soul,' she said, beating a hasty retreat, stumbling over the bag her unwelcome caller had left in the hall. It was black and expensive and clearly very heavy. He'd probably stolen it and stuffed it full of the loot at a house he'd broken into earlier. 'Just stay put and the ambulancemen will be with you any minute.' She turned, put the front door on the latch so that whichever of the emergency services got there first could let themselves in, and bolted upstairs.

Bertie was intermittently bawling and stuffing his fist into his mouth. Jessie threw on the first things that came to hand and then she picked him up. He needed changing. The nappies were downstairs. In the kitchen. It figured.

★   ★   ★

Baby? Patrick grabbed hold of the edge of the sink and hauled himself to his feet, doing his best to ignore the thumping pain in his head, the rush of nausea. That was the smell. Warm milk, baby cream, talc, that stuff Bella had used to sterilise bottles. That was the scent that had eluded him. How could he have forgotten it?

He'd come back after the funeral and it had seemed to fill the house. It had taken him months to get rid of it. He'd got to the point where he'd thought he'd have to move. But in the end he'd realised that the smell existed more in his head than in reality. A faint ghost of his lost family that would forever haunt him. Moving would have been pointless.

Where the hell was Carenza? He clutched onto the sink for a moment while the kitchen spun around him, determined that whatever happened he wouldn't be sick. When he felt strong enough to risk opening his eyes, he discovered that he was being regarded suspiciously by a uniformed policeman.

'Thank God,' he said. 'Officer, there's a mad-woman in my house. She hit me with a cricket bat.'

'Why don't you sit down, sir? The ambulance will be here in just a moment.' He didn't need a second invitation to sink into the nearest chair. His trousers squelched damply beneath him. 'Maybe, while I'm waiting we could just deal with the details? If you feel up to it. Shall we start with your name?'

'Shouldn't you caution me?' he demanded.

'Just for the record, sir.'

He let it go. 'Dalton. Patrick Dalton.'

The man made a note. 'And your address?'

'Twenty-seven Cotswold Street.'

'That's this address, sir.'

'That's right. My name is Patrick Dalton and I live here,' he said, slowly and carefully. 'This is my home,' he added, just to make the point.

The man made a note, then turned

as the front door opened. 'The medics have arrived. We'll sort all this out later, sir, down at the hospital.'

Patrick recognised the calming tone of a policeman confronted with a man he thinks is crazy. A policeman covering himself with excessive politeness in case he was wrong. He considered telling the man that he was a barrister, a Queen's Counsel, and that he'd find him listed . . . But his head was throbbing too much to bother. Hospital first, explanations later.

Then he'd take great pleasure in telling that woman to take her baby and her cat and get out of his house — right after she'd told him where he could find Carenza.

★   ★   ★

'Would you like to tell me what happened, miss?' The policeman stood by impassively while Jessie tried to change Bertie with fingers that didn't seem capable of removing the peel-back

55

strips from the tapes of the disposal nappy.

She'd been calm, very calm under the circumstances, but reaction was about to set in and she was nothing but jelly. The policeman, seeing her difficulty, helped her out while she explained, haltingly, what had happened.

'Mr Dalton said you hit him with a cricket bat.'

'That's a lie!' Then she flushed guiltily as she saw the cricket bat still lying on the floor where he'd dropped it. 'Dalton? Is that his name?'

'Patrick Dalton. So he says. He has a very nasty gash on his forehead.'

'I know. I think he must have hit his head when he fell.' She picked up Bertie, cuddled him. 'From the noise, I can only assume he stepped on the cat and lost his balance, although what he hoped to find in the fridge I can't imagine.'

'You'd be surprised. The fridge and freezer are favourite places to hide valuables. Unfortunately the villains know that, although the gentleman did say that he lives here.'

'He said that to me, too. It's not true, you know. I rented the house from a Miss Carenza Finch. I only moved in today.' Bertie grizzled into her shoulder. 'Maybe he has a concussion.'

'Maybe.' The man cleared his throat. 'There's no sign of a break-in, though. I hope you don't mind me asking, but this wouldn't be a domestic situation would it?'

'Domestic?'

'A lovers' tiff that's got a bit out of hand?'

'Lovers' . . . ' Jessie stared at him open-mouthed, temporarily lost for words. 'Officer, I've never met that man before in my entire life. And if I meet him again it will be too soon. I told you, I moved in here today,' she explained. 'The owner was going abroad for the summer and needed someone to make the place look lived in, to take care of her cat, her plants. Is this a high-crime area?'

'Not particularly. Most people have burglar alarms. You have one yourself,' he pointed out. 'Was it switched on?'

'Well, no. Actually, it wasn't. I was tired, what with the baby . . . I just forgot. Maybe I forgot to lock the door, too.' He nodded, understandingly. 'Do you want to see the lease? It's on the table in the hall. Oh, and that man left a bag out there, too. Evidently this wasn't his first job tonight.'

The policeman glanced at the lease, made some notes and then picked up the bag. 'I'll leave you in peace, then, miss. Maybe you could come down to the station and make a statement in the morning?'

'Yes, of course.' More time-wasting, Jessie thought, with a groan. Why did the wretched man have to choose her house? She followed the policeman to the door. 'What will happen to Mr Dalton? If that's his real name.' He glanced at the bag with its airline labels and flipped one over. It read Patrick Dalton, but there was no address.

'Maybe he stole the bag,' she said. 'And the name.' *And if he hadn't?* If he was telling the truth? His eyes didn't have the look of a man who lied. But then Graeme had eyes that promised the earth and she'd believed him. She was no judge.

'Right, then. I'll leave you to put the little one back to bed. Don't forget the alarm, now,' he reminded her as he headed down the front steps.

'I won't.' There was no way she was going through that again, she thought as she closed the door and set the alarm.

But, supercharged with adrenalin, she wasn't going to get back to sleep. She cleaned up the mess in the kitchen, trying not to think about her good-looking burglar with the honest eyes. Or the way his body had felt beneath her. It wasn't easy and a touch desperately, she connected her computer and set to work.

* * *

'I don't know how much longer I can hold out, Kevin. I miss him so much.'

'Me too. Weird, isn't it? The quiet actually hurts my ears.'

'Do you suppose it's worked yet?'

'I shouldn't think so, sweetheart. They wouldn't just pitch her out onto the street, would they? Not just like that?'

'Wouldn't they?'

'We said we'd give it a week, Faye.'

'I'm not sure I can hold out that long. Suppose she can't cope? Suppose — ?'

'Jessie is the most capable woman I know, and she was brilliant with Bertie on Sunday.'

'Yes, but I was there on Sunday.'

'You left enough instructions to fill a baby book. And if she has any problems she'll . . . '

'She'll what?'

'She'll do what she always does. She'll call up someone on the internet. Come and have a cuddle.'

'That's what got us into this situation in the first place.'

It had been light for an hour when Bertie woke. Maybe she was beginning to get used to less sleep, or maybe it was just that she'd made serious headway with the project she was working on, or maybe it was just the fact that she had somewhere to live for a few weeks, but Jessie felt on top of the world as she bent over the cot and picked him up.

'Hungry, sweetheart?' He jammed his fist into his mouth and she laughed.

She put on the kettle, made a note to organise a replacement shelf for the fridge, then made tea for herself and a bottle for Bertie. There was a mark on the curved edge of the worktop. Was that where Patrick Dalton, if that was really his name, had banged his head? Had he hit it that hard? The thought made her feel queasy. Maybe she should visit him in hospital.

Oh, right. And take him some hothouse grapes while she was at it.

Maybe he was already in a police cell.

The thought gave her no pleasure. He hadn't looked like a burglar. He hadn't sounded like a burglar either, but a good start in life didn't necessarily mean a good end.

★   ★   ★

'I'm sorry, Mr Dalton, but under the circumstances my officers had no choice but to take Miss Hayes' word for what happened.'

'I imagine her word was nothing but the truth. As she saw it.'

'You won't be pressing charges, then?'

'What charges? Your man saw the lease, you said. My niece apparently let my house to the woman. I imagine she'll insist, with some justification, that she's the injured party.' He touched the dressing on his forehead and winced. 'I'll reimburse Ms Hayes and when she's gone I'll find Carenza and make sure she has a summer she won't forget in a hurry.'

'Yes, sir. Is that your bag?' The Deputy

Chief Constable nodded to a young constable, who picked it up. 'The very least I can do is offer you a lift home.'

* * *

The kitchen was clean; Bertie had had his bath and was taking a nap. She was going to take a shower, get dressed and, when he woke, she would put him in the buggy and walk down to the police station to make her statement. And find out if her burglar had recovered.

Not that she felt responsible. When he'd grabbed her ankle he'd frightened her out of her wits. But then, when she'd been lying on top of him, confronted by grey eyes that looked . . . what, exactly? Certainly not threatening. Bemused, perhaps. Shaken, maybe.

Well, she'd been feeling a little off-balance, too. And not just because he'd pulled her feet from under her.

Which was ridiculous. She wasn't ever going to put herself through that kind of misery again. Never.

She'd be fine once she'd had a good night's sleep.

The *en suite* bathroom was richly furnished, matching the bedroom, its warm colours comforting and restful. Jessie changed her mind about the shower and turned on the taps to fill the huge old-fashioned claw-footed tub.

She hadn't had time to unpack, but the bathroom was well stocked and she helped herself to a dollop of a deliciously woody-scented bath gel. Then, leaving the door wide open so that she could hear Bertie if he cried, she fastened her hair up in a band and slipped beneath the foam.

* * *

'You're sure you don't need help?' The DCC was deeply embarrassed that his officers had arrested Patrick Dalton for housebreaking. The man was not only a well-known barrister but one of the youngest ever to have been appointed Queen's Counsel. It had been an honest mistake, but Mr Dalton wasn't known to be forgiving of mistakes made by the police.

'I think I can handle it. But thanks for the offer. And as for last night, well, if you don't tell anyone, I promise I won't.'

'That's very generous of you, Mr Dalton.'

'I know.'

Disconcerted by such bluntness, he said, 'You're sure you don't want me to come in and explain the situation to Miss Hayes?'

'I think I can handle it. And I've always got yesterday's newspaper if she needs convincing.' The headline gave him no pleasure, but the photograph had convinced the local plod that he wasn't a villain. It would certainly come in useful if he needed to convince Miss Jessie Hayes of that fact.

Patrick tucked the newspaper under his arm and took his bag from the young constable. His head was throbbing but he walked briskly up the steps to his front door. He didn't ring the bell. He knew that would be the sensible thing to do, but if the lady put the chain on the door and refused to let him across the threshold he would be in an awkward situation.

Somehow he didn't think he'd ever live it down in the Inns of Court if he had to resort to the law to remove an unwanted tenant. Which was why he wasn't going to risk it. Instead he waited until the police car had pulled away from the kerb and then let himself in.

The alarm was set this time. He set down his bag, tossed yesterday's evening paper on the hall table and punched in the code. There was no instant cry of outrage.

'Hello? Anyone there?' he called.

No reply. He made his way, cautiously, down to the kitchen, which had been restored to some semblance of normality.

He took in the painfully familiar sight of soaking baby bottles and for a moment, just a moment, was transported back ten years. Then the cat stropped against his legs. Scrub normality, he thought as he grimly made his way back up through the house. But there was no sign of his tenant. Apart from a milky footprint in the hall.

Maybe she was out. Taking the baby for a walk.

He realised he'd been holding his breath for far too long and he made a conscious effort to relax as he picked up his bag and climbed the stairs, determined on a shower and eight hours' sleep.

He was brought up sharply by the sight of the small cot standing beside the bed. Then he turned away, promising himself he'd have it folded and standing by the front door before she got back. Have a cheque and a van waiting. Maybe she'd be reasonable.

He thought about the determined way she'd been holding the cricket bat, even though she'd clearly been scared witless, and decided it was unlikely. But it was worth a try.

He kicked off his shoes, tugged his

shirt over his head as he stepped through the bathroom door, tossing it with practised aim into the laundry basket. Then he turned and came to an abrupt halt.

Jessica Hayes was lying back in the bath, damp chestnut curls clinging softly around her forehead and cheeks, islands of soft foam offering nothing but the minimum of decency to cover the enticing curves of her naked body.

Last night he'd been confronted by a harridan with a cricket bat. Minus the owl-like spectacles and the frown, she looked quite different. And totally vulnerable. It was a sight to soften the hardest of hearts.

His was well known to be made of tempered steel; he found it easier if people believed that. But, even so, if a man was going to come home and find a woman in his bathtub, he acknowledged, he'd have to go a long way before he found anyone who filled it quite so fetchingly.

However, he could quite understand

that, viewed from her perspective, the situation wouldn't seem quite as pleasurable.

On the contrary, he was certain that the only reason she wasn't screaming her head off right this minute was because she was fast asleep.

3

Patrick took a step back. Morally, he was perfectly within his rights to be in his own bathroom. He hadn't let his house. Jessie Hayes was the one who had no right to be there. She might have signed a lease, but he couldn't believe she'd really thought his house belonged to an eighteen-year-old girl whose idea of elegance was purple hair and a stud through her nose. All she had to do was look around her. The evidence, to anyone with half a brain, was obvious.

Unfortunately, the tabloid press wouldn't bother about that. The slightest hint of this situation and people would be dredging up the past and conversations would grind to a halt when he walked into a room — not, this time, because people didn't know what to say, but because they were saying too much.

That crack on the head must have been a lot harder than he'd realised, or he'd never have got himself into such a predicament. Finding a naked woman in his bath, though, had a way of concentrating his mind on the basics, and now he had just one objective in view: to get himself out of the house without her ever knowing he'd been in it.

Except his shirt was in the laundry bin. He had others, but if she saw it — and she would see it the minute she dropped her towel in there — she'd know . . .

He hadn't taken his eyes off her, not for a second, certain that even a blink would wake her. But she hadn't stirred. She was dozing peacefully, her eyes closed — dark, sea-coloured eyes, he remembered, not quite green, not quite blue, like the Mediterranean in a good mood. Then he wondered how he'd noticed such a thing in the mayhem of last night. Through the owl-like spectacles.

Maybe while she was lying on top of him, his subconscious volunteered, helpfully. He backed away from the thought, yet with the image before him he could instantly recall the warmth of her body against his, the feel of her hair as it brushed against his cheek. It tingled now, as he remembered, and he raised his hand as if to brush away an unwelcome sensation; then snatched his fingers back before they could.

Her lips were slightly parted, soft and pink and innocent of lipstick, and her arm was draped over the edge of the bath, totally relaxed by the warmth.

The tempered-steel jacket about his heart buckled slightly.

Then, as the drifting islands of foam moved, he saw the tiny tattoo of a ladybird on her thigh. And his body stirred, responding without hesitation to an overload of stimulation. The shock of it fixed him to the spot, his mind spinning with thoughts of a warm mouth beneath his, a warm body ready for love, and he gasped out loud as he realised that it wasn't a memory but this woman he was responding to.

She sighed softly as the cooling water began to disturb her. For a moment he remained where he was, transfixed by the image. But he really did have to move, get out of the bathroom, out of the house, before she woke and he gave her the fright of her life.

Even as he reached for the basket, a baby began to mewl.

He hadn't looked in the cot, had determinedly avoided doing so. And anyway, with Jessie Hayes out of the house, it would have been empty. His mistake. On both counts.

The whimpering grew louder, more insistent, drilling painfully into the shell that surrounded his heart, stopping him in his tracks. He was besieged from both sides by a rush of all the emotional cues he took such care to avoid. But here, at home, where he'd felt safe, his guard was down.

She sighed again, disturbed by the baby's cry and, abandoning any hope of recovering his shirt, he backed out of the danger zone. Even as he stepped out of sight of the bathroom door he heard a movement, the rush of water as she sat up. He tried not to think about that. A Botticelli *Venus* in his bathroom threatened the kind of sensory overload his body lacked any recent practice in handling.

'Hold on, Bertie.' He remembered the voice. Last night it had been tense, shaking with fear and outrage; now it was sweet and relaxed as she splashed noisily out of the bath. Bertie was not appeased.

Patrick turned unwillingly to confront the source of the noise. The infant, his little face screwed up in anguish, was reaching for him, arms held out, needing to be held, comforted, and instinct overrode the need to flee. Instead, he reached for the child, picked him up, tucked him against his shoulder in that never-to-be-forgotten gesture of comfort.

Bertie stopped crying and looked at

him, then grabbed his cheek with his chubby little hands and smiled. The tempered steel melted into a warm puddle.

Jessie, reaching for a towel, paused as Bertie stopped crying, and smiled. Things were looking up. 'There's a good boy. I'll be right with you.' She'd got some work done, she'd had a little nap in the bath and Bertie was getting used to her, responding to the sound of her voice. She might even get some unpacking done at this rate. 'Shall we go for a little walk when I've changed you?' she asked, helping herself to a bathrobe that was hanging behind the door. It was on the big side. Too big to have belonged to Carenza. But it was soft and comfortable. She wrapped it around her, pulling the belt tight to hold it up. 'I have to go to the police station and make a statement and then we could go to the park . . . ' She rubbed her face against the soft sleeve of the robe. 'Are you thirsty? Or do you want . . . ' She came to an abrupt halt in the bedroom doorway. The burglar was back and she'd been right last night. Vertical, he was very big indeed.

'Don't scream,' he said quickly. 'Please don't scream.' She shut her mouth with a snap that made her teeth wince. No scream. No way. He didn't have to repeat himself. He didn't even have to be so polite about it. He was holding Bertie and she would do exactly what he said. 'I'm not going to hurt you.' She tried to respond with something reassuring. Her mouth opened but her throat refused to co-operate. 'He was crying. I picked him up because he was crying. Do you want to take him?'

She nodded. No heroics this time, Jessie. She had to keep very calm and act as if everything was absolutely normal. Do nothing that would startle the man, or make him think she was a threat.

Calm. She rubbed sweaty palms down the sides of the towelling robe, feeling suddenly hampered by its size. If she had to make a dash for it, she'd undoubtedly trip over . . . Except, of course, that she wouldn't be dashing anywhere. Bertie was far more important than her own safety. *How on earth had he got in?*

Calm. Matter-of-fact. *Why had he come back?* To finish the job? There must be something worth a lot of money in the house if he'd risk it. She knew she should smile but her face wouldn't co-operate, either. It was frozen with fear.

Smile, she had to smile! She mustn't, under any circumstances, startle the man, let him see that she was afraid. She could do it for Bertie. Somehow she cranked the corners of her mouth into place and, ungluing her tongue from the roof of her mouth, she took a careful step forward.

'Y-yes.' Damn the nervous stuttering.

Patrick was horrified. What on earth had he done? The girl was absolutely petrified and who could blame her? 'He was crying,' he said again, gently.

'Please give him to me,' she begged, holding out her arms for her precious infant.

'Here, look. Go to your mummy.' He placed the baby in her arms but they were shaking so much he was afraid she might drop him. He continued to hold her and the baby. 'Have you got him?' She looked up at him, eyes wide. 'Maybe he needs changing,' he prompted.

'He usually does,' Jessie said. Then, catching a half-laugh that she recognised was close to hysteria, 'Did you escape?'

'What?' The robe she was wearing was soft against his chest. Her hair, descending from the band she'd tied it with to keep it out of the bath, smelt sweet and fresh and he wanted to stay there for a while. Then he realised what she'd said, that she must have a very different view of the situation. 'Oh, no . . . Look, have you got him safe?'

'Yes,' she said. But the burglar was blocking the way to the door. 'His things are downstairs.'

'Are they? Why?'

'Because I haven't had time . . . ' She stopped. She was not going to apologise to a burglar for her sloppy child-care practices. 'It's none of your damn business.' That made him smile, which was something. 'Can I get by?'

'Oh. Right.' He stepped aside. It occurred to Jessie that he wasn't wearing a shirt. He might be a burglar, she might have forsworn men, but that didn't prevent her from recognising a prime specimen when she saw one. Even without her spectacles. She didn't need them to appreciate the light sprinkling of dark hair across his chest, muscle definition that suggested a healthy attitude to fitness and shoulders capable of bearing the troubles of the world . . .

No shirt? Her mind snapped back into gear. Or shoes. He must have got away at the hospital. At least he'd waited for treatment, judging by the paper stitches on his forehead. Then he'd made a run for it. The police were probably looking for him right now. The police . . . she had to phone the police . . . But in the meantime she must act as if everything was perfectly normal.

She didn't want to do anything to startle him. 'They, um, didn't keep you in hospital?'

'They wanted to. I discharged myself.' Her face was so expressive, Patrick thought. He could see the train of thoughts as she tried to work out what had happened, could see the moment when she decided to force herself to act as if it was within the scope of her everyday experience to find a strange man, a shirt-less strange man, in her bedroom.

His bedroom.

Maybe it was. That baby had come from somewhere, although Mr Hayes was noticeable only by his absence. Maybe there wasn't a Mr Hayes. Or maybe he'd been kicked into touch. Or beaten to death with a cricket bat . . .

'Was that wise?'

Under the circumstances, probably not. But she was lovely. The infant completed her, just as Bella had seemed even more lovely with their baby in her arms. 'I don't much care for hospitals,' he said abruptly, stepping back to let her by. Then, 'Can you manage?' he asked, still anxious about the possibility of her dropping the child.

'Of course I can manage,' she snapped. 'I can't hang around waiting for a passing burglar — '

'Actually, it's breaking and entering during the day — '

'Or a barrack-room lawyer, come to that. Why don't you just get on with whatever . . . whatever it is you came to do?' She took a rather shaky breath. So much for calm. 'I'll pretend I didn't see you. Honestly.'

It occurred to Jessie that perhaps that wasn't the most tactful word to have chosen.

It occurred to Patrick that she was humouring him, that she was prepared to let him get on with whatever felonious business he had in mind so long as he didn't hurt the baby. Sensible, as well as gutsy. If he had broken in it would have been the wisest thing to do. While he applauded her sense, the situation did have a certain black humour to it. 'Are you offering to look the other way while I help myself to the Georgian silver?' he asked, trying not to laugh.

'Silver?' She hadn't seen any Georgian silver. But then, she hadn't been looking. 'Help yourself. I'm sure it's adequately insured,' Jessie said in her most reassuring voice as she took another step towards the door.

'Thanks,' he said. 'You're very kind, but the only thing I was planning on taking was a shower.'

'A shower?' She was staring at his chest and Patrick suddenly felt very naked; he had to make a conscious effort not to think about how she'd looked, lying back in his bath tub. That sexy little tattoo. 'Oh! A shower!'

'If, that is, you've left any hot water?' he asked, by way of distraction.

'I . . . um . . . yes . . . at least . . . probably . . . ' She looked confused now, as well she might. But there was no point trying to explain now. She clearly wasn't going to believe a word he said. 'There are plenty of towels and

I think I saw a razor in the cupboard, if you need . . . ' she went on, then stopped, clearly wishing she hadn't mentioned his spare razor.

'And then,' he said, 'I was going to catch up on some much needed sleep.'

'Sleep?' She swallowed, and for a moment he thought perhaps she was going to offer to change the sheets.

'I've had a very bad day, followed by a very bad night.'

'Snap,' she said, but gestured in the direction of the bed. 'But don't mind me. Help yourself.'

While she went downstairs and called the police like any concerned citizen. Well, that was fine with him. They'd put her in the picture and then they could sort out the lease. Which would undoubtedly cost him a great deal of money. Privacy was an expensive commodity.

Once she reached the safety of the doorway, she turned, her lip caught between her teeth. Then she said, 'Look, I have to know. How did you get in again?'

'The same way as I did last night. I used a key.'

'A key?' For a moment she was lost for words. Only for a moment, though. 'But I switched the alarm on after the police left last night. I know I did.'

'Yes, but you kindly left the code number on the note-pad by the phone. If I'd really been a burglar, I'd have been very grateful. Any more questions?'

She had dozens, he could see it in her face, but she clearly thought better of asking them. 'I'd better go and change Bertie.'

'You do that. And, since you're in a generous mood, why don't you put the kettle on and make some coffee?'

'Aren't you afraid it will keep you awake.'

'It's not for me. It's for the police. I assume you're going to call them and they'll be glad of a decent cup when they arrive. You wouldn't believe the stuff they serve in the local nick . . . '

She didn't hang about after that. And neither did he. He hadn't been kidding about needing a shower. But he was putting sleep on hold until he'd sorted out his problem tenant. She'd disturbed him more than enough and, when he woke up, he wanted to be sure he had his house to himself.

* * *

She heard him turn on the shower but he was bluffing; she knew he was bluffing. He planned to snatch whatever he'd come for and be gone long before any police arrived. Well, she'd see about that. Real burglar! He looked pretty real to her! Breath-stoppingly real.

She put Bertie down and grabbed for the phone, knocking a newspaper to the floor. Bertie grabbed for it, but as she kicked it out of his reach she realised that the face staring up at her from the front page was heart-stoppingly familiar. She didn't have her glasses, but the headline was about a big-news fraud trial in the Far East somewhere. Squinting at the caption, beneath a formally posed portrait that hadn't come from any police file, she could just make out the words 'PATRICK DALTON QC.'

The name on the bag she'd tripped over last night. The name her burglar had given the police.

She slowly replaced the receiver, stared at Bertie for a moment. Then she remembered that he needed changing and, putting the newspaper back where she'd found it by the phone, she stooped to pick him up.

She changed him on automatic. Put him in his high chair. Cleaned up. Washed her hands. Then made a pot of coffee. She suspected she was in trouble. Deep trouble. Her intruder had said that this was his house. She hadn't taken much notice because he'd had a knock on the head. Now she was very much afraid that he'd been telling the truth. That Carenza Finch was not the householder, had no right to sublet to her.

As if that wasn't bad enough, the rightful owner of the property was

Patrick Dalton *QC*. A lawyer and a very long way from the barrack-room variety. About as top of the tree in the lawyer stakes as it was possible to get, in fact. Short of being a judge.

And she'd thought that irritating the Taplow Towers Residents' Association had been trouble. At this rate she might just set up some kind of record for eviction.

She groaned out loud as she remembered the way she had encouraged him to help himself to the valuables. Promised not to tell. And he'd just stood there and let her make a fool of herself. No wonder he'd been smiling.

Taplow Towers Residents' Association, she suspected, were pussy-cats compared to Patrick Dalton. She had the unsettling feeling that Mr Dalton, with a dent in his cranium, would turn out to be pure tiger. Thank goodness for the lease. It proved . . . something.

She gave Bertie a rusk to chew on, poured herself a cup of coffee and wondered about Carenza Finch. She was young, and a bit funky, but she hadn't had the appearance of someone who'd squatted in the place and let it as a scam. Then she thought about the way she'd asked for the rent in cash and groaned. Who was she kidding?

Mao rubbed against her legs, demanding breakfast.

No, wait. There was Mao. Carrie had left her pampered cat behind. It was the only thing she'd been truly bothered about. Relief swamped her. It wasn't a squat and Carenza Finch wasn't just some girl taking advantage. At least, not of her. She'd been left to look after Mr Patrick Dalton's lovely house and precious plants when all she'd wanted to do was cross the channel with her friends.

Maybe, just maybe, if Patrick Dalton had left Carenza in charge of his house and she'd sublet it, her own position would not be as hopeless as she'd feared. What she needed, she thought, was a lawyer.

She pulled a face. She had a lawyer. *In situ*. And with that thought filling her mind she turned to see the man in question standing in the kitchen doorway.

The cup wobbled on its saucer.

He was impressive enough in an old grey T-shirt and jogging pants, his hair wet from the shower. In a black gown and horsehair wig, he'd undoubtedly frighten the life out of anyone he was prosecuting. Except he probably didn't bother with prosecution cases. There was a lot more money to be made defending villains than sending them to jail. Oil paintings by Stubbs and Georgian silver did not come cheap.

Which should make her feel better, but didn't much. But it gave her a little hope. The law might not be on her side, but it took its time. Maybe not three months, but long enough. He wasn't a burglar, after all, but a Queen's Counsel with a reputation to protect. He couldn't risk taking short cuts. With that thought to bolster her confidence, she managed a slightly wobbly smile. 'Do sit down, Mr Dalton. Help yourself to coffee.'

'I see they've explained the situation,' he said.

'They?' She found it easier to concentrate on mopping the dribble from Bertie's chin than look him in the eye. 'Who?'

'The police.' He sat down, poured himself a cup of black coffee and loaded it with sugar. 'I imagine you called them the moment you came downstairs?'

She glanced up at him. 'Actually, no. I was about to when I saw yesterday's newspaper. You made headlines last night, but not, it would appear, for breaking and entering.' And this time the smile came much more easily. 'But then, Patrick Dalton QC doesn't often lose.' It was a guess, but it must have been pretty close to the truth because he frowned.

'I didn't lose. My client decided at the last moment that his best interests were served by pleading guilty.'

He didn't sound too pleased about that. 'You're angry with him for doing the right thing?'

'Of course I'm angry. He was

innocent — ' Then he shrugged. 'Innocent of that particular charge at any rate. It would appear that he's been well paid to play patsy, though. His evidence would have embarrassed a lot of very powerful people.'

He cut a couple of slices from her loaf and dropped them into the toaster. 'I suppose Carenza asked you to stay here to look after the house while she went backpacking?'

'Not exactly.' He glanced at her. 'I've got a properly drawn up lease. And I've paid three months' rent in advance.'

'Oh, great. You've financed her holiday. Thanks,' he said sarcastically. 'Perhaps you would be kind enough to explain what you did to my sister?'

'Your sister?'

'Carenza's mother,' he explained. 'Carrie was supposed to be revising for A-level resits in the autumn.'

'If she's that bothered, your sister should keep a closer eye on her,' Jessie retaliated.

'How pleasant to discover one subject

on which we are in total agreement. But no matter. You can stop the cheque, we'll tear up the lease and that'll be an end to it.'

God, but he was arrogant. Bone-deep arrogant. He was being put to some inconvenience and it didn't matter a jot about her. Or Carenza. 'That would be difficult,' she said with considerable pleasure. 'I paid her in cash.'

'In cash?' Well, that wiped the satisfied look right off his face. 'You paid her three months' rent in *cash*?'

'Four. One month's rent as a deposit.'

'You didn't think that was a little odd?' he demanded.

She hadn't been ecstatic about the deal, but she hadn't been in a position to argue. 'There wasn't time for a cheque to clear. She was in a hurry.'

'I'll bet. I imagine she's already in France.' Jessie did not deny or confirm this. Carrie had mentioned a ferry. It had probably been going to France, but there were other options and it wasn't any of her business. She certainly had no intention of helping him find the girl. 'I suppose she thought I wouldn't find out,' he added.

'If your client had taken your advice, you probably wouldn't have.'

The toast popped up. He got up, crossed to the fridge and opened it cautiously, stared at the damage without expression. 'It doesn't matter.' He turned to her, butter-dish in hand. 'I'll reimburse you.'

She didn't think he was talking about the butter. 'There's no need. I don't want your money.'

'That's very generous of you, but I can't expect you to suffer because my niece — '

'You don't understand. I'm not being generous, Mr Dalton. And I don't intend to suffer. There's no need to reimburse me, because I'm not moving. I signed a proper lease, with an agency, and I've no intention of tearing it up. The policeman who came last night looked at it, took down all the details,' she said. Just in case he had any idea of tearing it up himself.

His eyes held her gaze; they were grey and steady and probably gave witnesses nightmares, but she wasn't in a court of law being cross-examined by him, so she refused to be intimidated. Well, not much.

To make the point, she helped herself to a slice of his toast. After all, it was *her* bread and her butter.

'I would have thought, under the circumstances, he might have passed on all the details.' Then, because she didn't want to make an enemy of him, she offered him a graceful way out. 'Maybe you're still a bit concussed. It does things to the memory.'

Patrick sat down and regarded her thoughtfully. 'There's nothing wrong with my memory.' His memory was in full working order and taking him on a distracting rerun of how she'd looked lying stretched out in his bath.

'Are you sure? Maybe a couple of nights in hospital would be safer.'

'Quite sure.' He found a use for the

smile that was desperately trying to break through. 'Besides, I believe that home is the best place for whatever ails you.'

'But this is *my* home for the duration of my lease,' she persisted. 'Surely you have someone you could stay with?' She was quite sure that one word from him would have women lining up. 'Family, or friends who would put you up for the next three months?'

The smile disappeared as easily as it had come. 'Three months!'

Oh, dear. He was upset. Jessie was surprised that he'd let her see how much. She was sure that if he'd been in court he wouldn't have raised his voice above a polite conversational tone, the kind that would have fooled a witness into believing he was chatting to a friend. Until it was too late.

Maybe he had a headache. She sympathised. He could have any amount of her sympathy. But not his house. Her house.

'What about you?' he demanded.

'Haven't you got any 'friends' or 'family' you could stay with?'

'If I'd had somewhere else, I wouldn't be here. I was at my wits' end when the agency offered me this.'

'What agency?'

She told him. 'I dealt with them on the phone. With Sarah,' she added, so that he would see that she was serious about this. 'They were incredibly efficient. Maybe they could help you,' she added. 'I'm far too busy to spend time looking for somewhere else.'

'Busy? You call sleeping in the middle of the morning busy?'

'Sleeping?'

'You've just had a bath. At least, I imagine that's what you were doing in the bathroom,' he said, rapidly back-tracking to retrieve his slip. 'Since you're wearing my bathrobe.'

Jessie glanced down at the robe she was wearing, horribly aware of a sudden heat in her cheeks. 'Is this yours?' she asked with studied carelessness. 'It's very comfortable.'

'I know.'

The thought that he'd been the last person to wear the towelling next to his skin didn't help with the cool façade she was intent upon. In fact she was beginning to feel desperately warm. But she made a real effort. 'It was a somewhat belated bath. My routine has been seriously disrupted by Bertie's arrival.'

'That's to be expected,' he said, less than sympathetically. 'You should have taken it into consideration when you embarked upon motherhood.'

'Oh, but — '

'This is my home, Jessie.'

'Oh . . . you remembered my name.'

'Yes, I remembered.' Would he ever forget?

She felt her cheeks heat up. 'Ms Hayes will do just fine,' she snapped.

'Carenza had no authority to sign a lease, Ms Hayes. It's absolutely worthless.'

'I think I'd like to check that out with a lawyer, if you don't mind.'

He glared at her. 'Do what you like, but I'd advise you to save your money. You can believe me when I tell you that, but for the fact that you've got a baby, I'd have you out on the street today.' Jessie, who'd been on the point of explaining that Bertie wasn't her baby when he'd distracted her, decided that it would be wiser to keep that fact to herself for the time being. 'Shall I call your precious agency?' he offered. 'If they're so efficient they should be able to find you somewhere else to live — '

'Don't bother.' Being given twenty-four hours' notice once was unpleasant, twice in the same week brought all those impetuous, reckless traits she'd been working so hard to keep under control bubbling to the surface. 'I'm not moving.'

There was the briefest pause before he said, 'Then we've both got a problem, Ms Hayes, because neither am I.'

For a moment the room seemed to hum with tension, then Jessie swallowed hard and, refusing to be intimidated, she said, 'Well, I suppose I could offer you a sublet on the boxroom. It was a bit of a strain paying Carenza the whole rent in advance — '

He seized on this. 'You can have it back. All of it. And a month's rent as compensation for your trouble. I'll write you a cheque — '

She didn't want a cheque. She didn't want to move. Why the devil should she? 'It's not furnished, of course, and the guest bathroom is a bit basic,' she continued, as if he hadn't interrupted. 'Maybe you've a Z-bed or something stashed in the attic?' He neither confirmed nor denied this. He seemed totally lost for words. 'Would that be a suitable compromise?' Then Mao, still hungry, rubbed against Patrick's leg. He moved it irritably. Mao persisted. 'I'm sure we could come to some arrangement about sharing expenses,' she added.

If she'd hoped to provoke him, she had succeeded. He erupted from the chair. 'I'm sharing nothing, Ms Hayes, so you'd better start looking for somewhere else right now while I'm prepared to be reasonable! And you can take your cat with you!'

This was his idea of reasonable? 'You'll give me time to put some clothes on before you throw me onto the street?'

Brought up short, he appeared to take his time considering his answer. Bundled up in his bathrobe, her hair caught up in a little stretchy hair tie, her face pink and shiny from the bath, Jessie had no illusions about her sex appeal, but apart from the fluffy white towelling robe all she was wearing was her skin.

Reminding him that she was quite naked, she realised too late, had been needlessly reckless.

4

Patrick swallowed. His bathrobe, too big for her by yards, gaped invitingly to expose the creamy skin at her throat, to hint at the soft rise of her breasts. If anything the mystery was more enticing than her unwitting exposure. His mind filled in the lovely curves, the sexy little ladybird, and the dull ache that had been gnawing at him since he'd walked into the bathroom and discovered her there intensified and quickened.

Jessie, her face hot, quickly turned, picked up Bertie and held him, an innocent shield against her own impetuous tongue. She'd thought she had it under control, along with her mind and her heart. Memo to brain. Must try harder. In the meantime she firmly quashed any inclination to feel guilty about letting Patrick Dalton believe that Bertie was her baby.

She knew it was wrong. In theory. But in practice he'd made the situation very plain: if she owned up to simply minding Bertie as a temporary measure while her brother and sister-in-law had caught up on their sleep, he wouldn't hesitate to put her out on the street. He was certainly big enough to pick her up and carry her there, and, once outside, she would be the one who'd have to sue to get back in, which would serve no point at all, since she'd still need somewhere to live in the meantime.

Worse, he might invoke some arcane law that dealt very harshly with parents who put sleep before duty. Kevin and Faye knew they could trust her, but social services might take a very dim view of her lack of credentials for even temporary motherhood.

'I'll own up to the baby, Mr Dalton,' she said, carefully neither confirming or denying that Bertie was hers. 'But I'm afraid Mao is nothing to do with me. He belongs to Carenza.'

'Oh, sh — ' he bit back the word as

Bertie smiled up at him ' — sugar,' he said.

'Mmm.' He didn't care for cats either, she could see. Which was handy. 'Actually, I think he's hungry. Maybe you'd like to mash some fish for him? It is cooked. You just have to go through it with your fingers to check for bones.' He didn't answer and Jessie had the feeling that, for once in his life, Patrick Dalton was at a loss for an answer. She opened the fridge and, trying very hard not to display her own gagging distaste for the job, she carefully sifted the fish through her fingers before tipping it into Mao's dish. 'You see,' she said, pressing home this unexpected advantage.

The cat ceased stropping himself against Patrick's legs and crossed to examine her offering. He sniffed, looked up at her in disgust then, flicking up his tail, crossed to the kitchen door and waited for someone to open it for him.

Jessie felt like applauding. He couldn't have performed better if she'd coached him. Instead she opened the door and, with a sigh, said, 'I guess it'll have to be minced chicken today.' She turned to see how he'd taken it, but Patrick Dalton was already halfway up the stairs.

'Mr Dalton,' she called after him.

He paused, half turned. 'What?'

'If you're going to take a nap, I'd like to — ' She'd like to get dressed first. Her brain clearly wasn't taking calls. Fortunately he didn't wait to hear what she wanted.

'A nap! You think I feel like sleeping? I've never felt more awake in my entire life and I'm going out. In the meantime you'd be well advised to start looking for somewhere else to live.'

'Or what?' she asked.

'Or — or I'll do it for you.'

Well, that was one answer, she supposed, but he didn't wait for her approval and a moment later the front door slammed shut on the floor above her.

'Round one to us, I think,' she whispered in Bertie's ear as she kissed his dark curls. 'It's a pity he's so upset, though.' She sighed. 'It's understandable, of course. Carenza has been a very naughty girl. She's betrayed his trust. Not,' she added, 'that he seemed particularly surprised about that.' She tickled Bertie's tummy and he giggled. 'It's no laughing matter, young man. You'd better not do anything like that to me when you're her age,' she said, laughing as she lifted him out of his chair. But as she tucked him against her shoulder, the soft skin of his cheek against her neck, the idea of being nothing more than an aunt, of never having this for herself, didn't seem so very funny.

Not funny at all, she thought, as she stopped at the front door to slip on the chain and reset the alarm to warn her of Patrick Dalton's return.

★ ★ ★

'Patrick, dear boy, come in! What on earth has happened to you?'

'Do I look that bad?' The words were redundant: his aunt's face warned him that he looked pretty much the way he felt. He dragged his fingers through his hair, encountered the stitches. 'Don't answer that. Look, is this is a bad time, Aunt Molly? I know I should have called first — '

'Not at all. And Grady will be overjoyed to see you. He's dozing in the garden. Why don't you go through and give him a surprise while I put the kettle on?'

He followed her through to the kitchen and glanced out of the window at the lean, shaggy old hound lying in the shade of an apple tree. 'How's he been?'

'Perfect. A lamb. They say you can't teach an old dog new tricks, but he's as sharp as a button still. We've had a great time . . . ' She stopped as she turned from the sink. 'I saw the paper but I assumed you'd been sleeping off the jet lag today.'

'Sleep's on hold for the moment.'

'Don't leave it too long,' she advised. Then, 'Well? Are you going to tell me what happened?'

'This?' He made a vague gesture in the direction of the dressing. 'It's nothing. I tripped over a cat.' He took the coffee she poured, added sugar.

'A cat?' Her expression conveyed a certain scepticism, but she let it go. 'Maybe you should have a drop of whisky in that and stretch out in the spare room for a hour or two.'

'The offer is almost irresistible . . . ' he yawned, rubbed his hands over his face ' . . . but I'd better stick to coffee. I've got a problem that needs a clear head.'

'A legal problem? Anything I can do?'

'Unfortunately there isn't. Carenza decided that looking after my house for the summer was a bit of a bore, so she's let it to some woman and pocketed the money to go walkabout in Europe.'

'Wretched child. She assumed you wouldn't find out, I suppose.'

It was what the cricket-bat-wielding

Venus had thought, but he knew Carenza better than that. 'She'd have owned up, Molly. I imagine she thought that, provided nothing dreadful happened, I'd applaud her initiative. The trouble is, she's probably right.'

'Ah, well, you always did indulge her.'

He shrugged. 'Maybe I do, but someone has to. Her father doesn't make much of an effort and Leonora's always too busy. On this occasion, though, I was trying to be tough.' Big mistake. 'If I'd indulged her, I wouldn't be in this mess.'

'I suppose you'll have to buy her off? Carenza's tenant?'

'I've tried. Her riposte was to offer to sublet me my own spare room. If I couldn't find anywhere else to stay.' Despite his annoyance, he found himself grinning as he recalled her cheek. She was a lot more than just a pretty face. A lot more. 'For a reasonable rent.'

'You're kidding me!'

He straightened his face. It wasn't the least bit amusing. She had to go and the sooner the better. 'I wish. Any suggestions?'

'Stay here?'

'Aunt Molly, are you suggesting I accept defeat and give in gracefully?'

She laughed. 'No, I suppose that's too much to expect.' She considered for a moment. 'You could wait until she goes out and change the locks.'

'That's an appalling thing to suggest.' He put down his cup and grinned at her. 'Why didn't I think of it?'

'You mean, you haven't? That knock on the head must have been harder than you thought. More coffee?'

Patrick shook his head. Then rather wished he hadn't. He needed to lie down. Soon. 'Yes, well, she's got a lease. It might not be worth much, but I can't be seen to be disregarding her rights under the law.'

'And?' she prompted.

He shrugged. 'And she's got a baby.' He sketched Bertie's approximate size with his hands. 'A boy. About six months old.'

His aunt reached out, touched his arm briefly. Then she asked lightly, 'No man around?'

'Not so's you'd notice. No ring anyway.' And when had he noticed that? 'But marriage seems to have gone out of fashion.' Then he added, 'Ms Hayes didn't give me the impression of being a woman who needs a man to hold her hand.'

'One must have once been holding something.' Patrick thought about the way she had been stretched out in his bath. Holding her wouldn't be any kind of hardship, he conceded. None whatever. 'Right,' Molly said after a moment, when it became clear that he wasn't about to volunteer any further information, 'I guess it's going to be the boxroom, then. You said the rent was reasonable.'

'There's only one problem with that solution.' Apart from the boxes of memories he couldn't bear to look at, but couldn't bear to let go. 'It hasn't got a bed.'

Dame Justice Mary Faulkner grinned. 'You call that a problem? Most men would consider it an opportunity.' Then, more gently, she said, 'It's been nearly ten years, Patrick. Bella wouldn't have wanted you to be alone.'

'I know. But since I lost her — lost them both — I just can't seem to . . . ' He stopped, tried to marshal his thoughts. 'I see a woman and I think . . . what's the point? She's not Bella.' Until he'd seen his lovely tenant lying naked in the bath. That had been a revelation. 'It's not fair to burden any woman with that,' he said. And he stood up. 'I'd better be getting back.'

'Just in case your unexpected house guest doesn't have your scruples about changing the locks?'

'She wouldn't . . . ' he began, then stopped. He rather thought she might.

*　*　*

Jessie made the bed, tidied up the bathroom, tutting irritably at the heap of abandoned towels, and then emptied the laundry basket, separating her clothes from those of Mr Patrick Dalton QC.

She didn't take in washing. Or lodgers. No matter how attractive. And he was attractive. Very nearly as good-looking as Graeme. Which had to be bad news.

She looked at the pile of washing and picked up a man's shirt. Handmade in Jermyn Street, black, stiff with dried milk and egg; she would have guessed it belonged to her Learned Friend the QC, even if he hadn't been wearing it the last time she'd seen it. Except that he hadn't been wearing a shirt when she'd discovered him in her bedroom. His bedroom. Their bedroom. Oh, heck.

Anyway, she'd noticed he hadn't been wearing a shirt. It had been hard not to. His naked chest had filled her sightline. Broad, finely muscled, lightly tanned: his time in the Far East hadn't all been spent in court. Mouth-watering, in fact, as chests went . . . and definitely shirt-less.

Which was odd. At the time she'd

put it down to him having escaped from hospital, but presumably when he'd been driven home with grovelling apologies from the local constabulary for their mistake he'd been fully dressed. So how had it come to be under her towel, way beneath the rest of his clothes? Her frown deepened. She was missing something. Something important.

She yawned. Eight hours of undisturbed sleep. That's what.

Her reflections were interrupted by the clangour of the burglar alarm. Mr Dalton, it would appear, had returned.

Bertie woke and added to the mayhem. Jessie picked him up and, propping him on her hip, she walked downstairs. At least she could save time by cutting out her session at the gym this week. Up and down stairs . . . no time to eat . . .

The front door was open, but only by three or four inches. The length of the chain. She peered through the crack, prepared to be courteous if he stopped leaping to conclusions about making himself at home. Even if it was his home.

There was no one there. She was surprised he'd given up that easily. It made her nervous. But she closed the door then looked for the pad on which Carenza had written the reset code. It was gone. Great.

She shut her eyes and concentrated hard, trying to visualise the numbers, but the noise stopped as abruptly as it had begun and, startled, she opened them again. Patrick Dalton was standing beside her and, as he turned from the control panel, it happened again. The take-your-breath-away thing.

Forgetting to breathe was a bad sign. The lack of air to her brain made thinking hard. And when she wasn't thinking, her judgement was very suspect indeed.

She needed to get angry, point out that he was trespassing —

'Neat trick, Ms Hayes,' he said before she could launch into her outraged householder act. 'But there's no point putting the chain up on the front door if you don't secure the bolts at the back.'

He didn't wait for her response and after a moment, during which she was afraid she was making a fair impersonation of a goldfish, she followed him down the short flight of stairs to the kitchen, determined to give it to him anyway. He was filling a large bowl at the sink from the tap.

'You came through the garage,' she said.

'Not *the* garage. *My* garage. And I need you to shift your junk.'

'It's *my* garage,' she said firmly, catching her breath, and deciding that politeness would serve her better. That way she continued to occupy the moral high-ground. 'I've got a lease. And it isn't junk.'

It just looked that way. She'd had to pack quickly in whatever boxes the porter at Taplow Towers could find, and she'd dumped them in the garage until she could sort them out. She hadn't anticipated an irate lawyer requiring a place for his car. She didn't argue, though. They had enough to contend with without worrying about a few cardboard boxes.

After his earlier outburst, he too appeared to be making an enormous effort to be civil because he turned to face her before he said, 'Please . . . ' Good start, she thought. ' . . . don't be stubborn about this.'

Stubborn! She wasn't being stubborn, she was standing up for her rights. 'Under the circumstances, I consider that I'm being thoroughly reasonable,' she replied, sweet reason itself.

'Do you? In that case, under the circumstances, I consider it very reasonable to assume that if my car is clamped and towed away because it's parked in a restricted area, you'll pay the fine.' He checked his watch. 'You have twenty-two minutes starting from now.'

Every impulsive cell in her body was urging her to tell him what he could do with his twenty-two minutes. She restrained them. She didn't do impulsive any more.

At least that was the plan. It was being sorely tried, and required a fast count to ten before she enquired, with excessive politeness, 'And what do you suggest I do with my belongings in twenty-two minutes?'

'That, Ms Hayes, is your problem.'

'I see.' If that was how he wanted to play it, he would discover that she had problems to spare and was perfectly willing to share. 'And you want me to move the boxes now?'

'You've wasted two minutes already.'

'Very well.' She strapped Bertie into his high chair, considered giving him a rusk to chew, then decided against it. Jessie did not want Bertie happy.

'I'll be as quick as I can,' she said, picking up her handbag and heading upstairs towards the front door, 'but this will probably take a while.'

She had reached the third step before he caught on. 'Ms Hayes!'

'Yes?'

'Haven't you forgotten something?'

Jessie paused without looking back,

opened her handbag and said, 'Keys, credit cards, mobile phone. No, that should do it.' She took another step.

'Baby?' he said tersely.

'Bertie?' She turned then. Patrick didn't look at all happy. In fact he looked rather pale, strained. The impulsive Jessie wanted to put her arms around him, reassure him, tell him to go to bed and get some rest and she'd move right out . . .

'I can't move boxes and hold a baby, Mr Dalton,' she said, instead of doing just that. 'But don't worry, he's no trouble.' She didn't bother to cross her fingers when she said that. It was, after all, simply a matter of perception, and her perception, right now, was that Bertie was an absolute angel. 'And he seems to like you. Maybe you could take him for a walk later — '

Later? Later! 'But you can't just leave him . . . '

'After you've fed him?' she finished. The sudden reappearance of her marsh-mallow centre had been a close call.

'Fed him!'

'I'll have to put my things into storage somewhere, Mr Dalton. It shouldn't take more than an hour or two,' she added. 'Probably.' Then, 'If you'll just give him a jar of baby food and make a bottle . . . You'll find the instructions taped to the container. And you'll find the nappies in the cupboard beside the sink in the utility room. You do know how to change a nappy?'

'Are you being serious?'

'Perfectly serious.' She met his gaze and held out against the heat that seemed to be turning her insides to mush. It wasn't easy. 'Weren't you?'

He held up his hands. 'All right. Okay. I'll move the boxes. There's probably room at the back of the garage if I pile them up — '

'Oh, but . . . '

'What?'

'Nothing.' He waited, too sharp to be fooled into thinking she'd finished. 'You will be careful with the cartons containing my china . . . '

'Are they marked 'Fragile'?' he

enquired, with the dangerous look of a pressure cooker about to blow.

'I'm afraid not. And I didn't do a great job of packing. I moved in something of a hurry.'

'I wonder why,' he said sarcastically, 'when you're such a fun person to share a house with?'

She didn't dignify that with an answer. 'I'm sure you'll manage. If you just look inside each box to check so that you don't put anything on top of my Royal — '

'All right!' He was losing it, she thought. That blade-edged arrogance, honed on total confidence in his masculine superiority, was blunting nicely. 'All right,' he repeated, more carefully. 'I'll take care of your china. But no more games with the door chain and the alarm.'

'I promise,' she said.

Maybe she wasn't totally convincing. Or maybe years of courtroom experience had taught him to be wary of anyone who made a promise that easily, because he said, 'I'm sure you realise that Carenza had no legal right to sign a lease on this house, Ms Hayes. I'm sure a determined lawyer could have you evicted in days, if he wanted to be difficult.'

She didn't doubt it. Not for a minute. And he was a very determined lawyer. 'No more games with the chain,' she agreed. And this time she meant it. 'I'll even make you a cup of tea for your trouble.' Before you go, she added, but silently.

'Thank you,' he said, with a look that suggested he could read her mind. 'That would be very welcome.' He sounded as if he meant it, too, and it occurred to Jessie that he looked desperately weary as he returned to the sink, picked up the bowl of water. Guilt stabbed at her. This was his home. All he wanted was a little peace. Somewhere to fall down and go to sleep. Just like her.

'Mr Dalton — '

'Please . . . I think we've gone beyond such formality, Ms Hayes. It's Patrick . . . ' He didn't wait for her to snub him by refusing to reciprocate the gesture. Instead he turned away and put the bowl down just inside the kitchen door. 'Grady, here boy.' A dog rose from below the back-door step and began to drink with sloppy relish from the bowl. A huge dog. Big and shaggy, it reached the top of his thigh . . .

Jessie froze.

I hate cats and so does my dog. He'd said that when he'd been lying in the mess of eggs and milk on the kitchen floor. She hadn't taken any notice at the time, well not serious notice anyway, because she'd thought he was a burglar. But he hadn't been a burglar after all.

This was his house.

And *that* was his dog.

That was where he'd gone when he'd stormed out. Not to consult the local small ads for flats to let. He might have left Carenza in charge of his house, but he didn't trust her with his car, or his dog.

She'd thought that Mao was a nuisance. She'd thought having Patrick

122

Dalton as a lodger would be the pits and planned to use any means in her power — she was hoping for big things from Bertie, here — to discourage him from staying.

Now the full horror of the situation was borne in upon her.

Jessie whimpered and tried to shrink back into the wall. She didn't care for cats much, but she could tolerate them. Dogs . . . dogs were something else . . .

Patrick turned as he heard her strangulated cry, turned and knew in an instant that he had discovered her weakness. 'What is it? What's the matter?' he asked, but he knew. It didn't take any kind of a genius to work out that his tenant was scared . . . more than scared . . . absolutely petrified of his dog and in that moment he knew he'd won.

And lost.

She was flattened against the wall, scrabbling against it, as if she wanted to disappear into it, uttering small, incoherent cries of distress. This was a lot more than scared and, much as he wanted to be free of this disturbing lady and her infant, he could not be that cruel.

'It's all right,' he said carefully, reassuringly, 'he won't hurt you.' But even as he said the words he realised that she was beyond simple reason. He picked up the bowl and moved it outside. Grady looked up, quirked his shaggy eyebrows in surprise. 'Sorry, boy. Temporary arrangement.' And he pushed him outside and shut the door.

She seemed to slump against the wall, and before he could stop himself he was across the kitchen and holding her. 'Ms Hayes . . . ' God, that sounded so stupid when she was trembling in his arms, when he could feel the short, panicky breaths against his throat, smell the lingering scent of soap on her skin. 'Jessie . . . please, it's all right.' Still she clung to him, shivering with fear. 'You're safe. Really. He can't touch you. I've shut him outside.' Lost in her own world of fear, she wasn't hearing him, but he continued to murmur the kind of quiet, soothing words he'd use to comfort a child, to gentle a nervous horse.

The words didn't matter. It was the sound, the security of human touch that she sought, and he held her close, his lips brushing against her hair, her temple as he kept up a steady stream of reassurance that came from somewhere he hadn't been in a long time, a place deep inside him, bricked up with ice, beyond all risk of feeling.

All day she'd been battering at the glacier with her voice, her smile, and now, with her need to be held, protected. So when at last she stirred, shivered against him and looked up, her eyes huge, dark, disturbed — he forgot why he was holding her, forgot everything . . .

Jessie knew she'd made a fool of herself. She knew it was stupid to be so afraid, but knowing it didn't help. This did. Being held by Patrick, his voice murmuring reassurance in her ear, the sweet tenderness . . .

She looked up, tried to collect herself, explain. But looking up didn't help. Patrick's eyes were full of concern, warmth, the gold dominating the grey. And his mouth, made for passion, was made for tenderness too.

There was a moment of stillness, an infinitesimal moment when anything might have happened.

And then he kissed her.

It had been so long . . . He'd driven out of his mind the silky taste of a woman's mouth, the tender touch that could so swiftly boil over into something to scorch the soul.

Butterscotch and brandy, sweet and vital, Jessie's mouth breathed life into him, lit a torch that flamed in his blood, melted every last vestige of ice as it raced through his veins, heating and reviving desires that had been so long suppressed.

Jessie forgot why she was scared. Forgot every promise she had made herself on the subject of instant attraction, acting on impulse. There was nothing inside her head but the taste of Patrick's mouth, the scent of his skin, and for a long, blissful moment she left the real world and let herself be swept away . . .

'Jessie . . . ' She looked up and the fantasy evaporated. The kiss had been the stuff of fairy tales, perfect, ten out of ten without any need to practise. His face told a different story. He looked lost, desperate . . . Well, he was a lawyer. Maybe he thought she'd sue.

Patrick decided his brain must have blown a fuse when it had collided with the work surface. That had to be the answer; anything else was too appalling to contemplate — like looking into an abyss. Nothing, nothing would ever tempt him along a path that could lead to such pain . . .

'Jessie . . . ' He was trying to apologise, she realised. Even now his lawyerly brain was groping for an appropriate form of words. Well, damn him, she wasn't going to let him apologise for kissing her.

'Why did you do that?' she demanded.

'You were hysterical. You were frightening the baby.' Bertie, reacting to the sharpness in her voice, immediately began to whimper.

Hysterical? Had she been hysterical? Jessie closed her eyes, rubbed her hand against her forehead, then she shuddered. Yes, that had to be it. She'd made a total fool of herself. 'Good move,' she said, with an attempt at humour. 'It certainly worked.'

'Less brutal than a slap,' he agreed, matching her lightness. And when she opened her eyes again, she saw that his were simply concerned. Nothing more. She must have imagined the heat, the hot desire.

'It was the sh-shock. I didn't have time to prepare myself. I can cope if I know in advance . . . ' This was ridiculous. She ought to be standing up on her own two feet, not leaning against Patrick Dalton like some pathetic creature with no bones in her legs. If she kept this up he'd think she wanted

him to kiss her again. 'He's so b-big.'
Make that a *half-witted*, pathetic creature.

Patrick breathed a sigh of relief as the danger passed. As they returned to the role of two strangers. 'The bigger they are, the softer they are,' he said.

'The bigger they are, the bigger their teeth. What kind of dog is that?'

'Grady? He's an Irish wolfhound.'

'A wolfhound . . . ' she echoed, weakly.

'I'm sorry, Jessie. I should have warned you. I forget Grady can be rather overwhelming at first sight. He really is as gentle as a lamb. I promise.'

'Mmm. People always say that, don't they? Just before their gentle, wouldn't-hurt-a-fly dog sinks its teeth into your ankle.'

That sounded like experience talking. 'In Grady's case it's the truth, the whole truth and nothing but the truth,' he said, hoping to raise another smile.

'I'd prefer to see him swearing the oath, if you don't mind.'

'Look, he's eleven years old,' he said, seeking to reassure her. 'He might not need a Zimmer frame, but in dog terms that's pretty much an old-aged pensioner.' He ought to help her to a chair. Do something useful, like making her a cup of hot, sweet tea, but he didn't want to let go. She felt so good in his arms. She smelt wonderful. Like a walk in the woods. 'He belonged to my wife . . . ' He stopped. *My wife*. He couldn't remember the last time he'd used those words. 'She had him from a tiny puppy.' Then he smiled. 'Well, a puppy at any rate. For Christmas.'

'She left him with you, though.' She said it as if it was a cross to bear, he thought. And in a way it was.

'*We won't be long.*' *Bella had been standing in the study doorway. 'It's just Mary Louise's routine visit to the clinic. I can't take Grady, but he'll be company for you . . . '*

'How long has she been gone?'

'What?' He looked, Jessie thought, as if he'd been somewhere else, miles away. 'Oh.' He closed his eyes momentarily. She obviously thought he and Bella were

130

divorced — and he didn't enlighten her. 'Ten years. Nearly ten years.'

She reached out tentatively to touch his cheek, seeking to bring him back to her. 'You don't think that maybe the dog was a mistake?' Oh, God, she couldn't believe she'd said that! It was lack of sleep, fright . . . 'Forget I said that. Please.' She pulled away before he could. But he caught her hand, held it, his face creasing into the unfamiliar lines of a smile that had once been as natural to him as breathing.

'It's all right. Forget it. Can you make it to that chair now?'

'I th-think so.'

He'd smiled — even though she'd touched a nerve talking about Bella's dog like that. Patrick could scarcely believe it. But she hadn't meant to hurt him, she'd had a shock, hadn't been thinking straight. He'd been guilty of that himself, heaven help him, and if he'd blurted out what had happened, if he'd let her see she'd hurt him, Jessie would have been embarrassed, horrified

131

at what she'd said. She felt bad enough already, he could see. He owed her that smile and Bella, he felt, would have approved. 'Here, sit down. I'll get you a drop of brandy.'

'No. No, I don't . . . '

'Don't drink?'

'Don't like brandy.' She couldn't bear to look at him, afraid the smile hadn't been a smile, but a rictus of disgust. Instead she looked at the door. 'He can't get in, can he?'

'Not unless he's learned how to use a door handle while I've been away.' Then, because flippancy wasn't going to help, he hunkered down on his heels and looked up into her face. 'Are you scared of all dogs, or just big ones?'

'Um . . . all d-d-dogs.' Clearly just saying the word was bad enough. 'Although the small ones are probably the worst. Marginally.' Her foot twitched, as if remembering pain, and she reached down, rubbed at an old scar just above her ankle bone. A terrier of some kind, he thought, the kind that sinks its teeth

132

in and won't let go.

'Yes, I see. Well, I promise you that Grady doesn't bite. But I'll lock the back door before I go.'

'Go?' He was perfectly aware that in her embarrassment at a kiss that they both knew had gone far beyond anything called for by hysteria, her certainty that she'd said something unforgivable had meant she'd been avoiding meeting his gaze. At his reminder that he was going out, her head jerked up. 'Go where?'

Oh, Lord, but it would be so easy to drive her out, he thought. Let Grady in, write a cheque and she'd be in a taxi before the traffic warden came round to tell him that he'd better shift his car, pronto.

But no matter how much he wanted her to leave, he couldn't do it that way. 'Just to shift your boxes, get my car off the street before it's towed away.' He straightened, crossed to the door and turned the key. Grady would be happy enough for the time being, stretched out in the shade beneath the bench.

'There, it's locked.' Then, just in case this was all an act — because with the back door locked and the chain up at the front he'd have no way back in — he pocketed it. A woman with a child to protect will do anything. Anything.

She still didn't look happy. 'I'll be as quick as I can,' he said.

She didn't bother to remind him to be careful with her china. He didn't bother with a reminder not to put the chain up. Despite the key nestling in his pocket, he had the feeling that she wouldn't be moving from that chair any time soon.

Bertie, fed up that he wasn't the centre of attention, finally stopped threatening tears and turned them into reality.

'Oh, sweetheart, are you hungry? I'm so sorry!'

Patrick watched as she forgot her fear and swooped across the kitchen to kiss her precious baby, unfastening the harness so that she could pick him up

134

and make a fuss of him.

The sight of mother and child together drove him from the kitchen to take out his feelings on the in-animate objects cluttering up the garage.

He loaded and shifted and wondered about Jessie and her baby. She wore no ring, was almost certainly unmarried. So what had happened to Bertie's father? Was he still on the scene?

And why the devil did he care? One kiss meant nothing. 'Nothing,' he said, out loud, to emphasise the point. She was a complication that he couldn't handle. The baby just made things worse. She'd have to go.

★ ★ ★

Jessie was still shaking as Bertie finished one of the jars of goo his mother had sent for him by the case-load, along with yards of instructions on how much he should have and when. But whether it was the dog or his master that caused the tremor would have been hard to say.

The dog that had attacked her when she was a little girl had left faded scars on her foot, but there had been no permanent damage. Just the marks left by life. Nothing that she couldn't live with. Graeme had left emotional scars. Did her reaction to Patrick Dalton, the way she'd responded to his kiss, suggest that they were fading too? Just part of the learning process? Or was it just a warning that she hadn't learned a thing?

Hysterical? Had she really been hysterical? 'What do you think, sweetheart?' she asked Bertie, using the soppy voice that her perfectly intelligent sister-in-law employed when she was feeling particularly happy with her infant. She hadn't understood it — after all Bertie wasn't going to answer. But maybe three days of motherhood had changed her, because suddenly it all made perfect sense. Bertie seemed to like it, because he smiled back. She wiped his face, lifted him out of the chair. 'Oh, you think that's funny, do you?' She tickled him and he laughed.

That was when she realised why he was so happy. 'Bertie! Darling! You've got a tooth! Oh, God bless you!' She turned as Patrick Dalton put a box down on the kitchen table.

'This one,' he said, in a voice that suggested she had nothing to smile about, 'wouldn't fit.'

'Wouldn't it? Oh, well, maybe it could go upstairs, in that boxroom with the rest of the junk.' Then, because she was suddenly so pleased with life, with herself, with Bertie, and there was no one else to share her news with, she said, 'He's got his first tooth! Look!'

Patrick was unimpressed, keeping his distance, making no move to inspect this little miracle. 'Shouldn't you be sharing this once in a lifetime moment with his father?' he asked.

Jessie flamed furiously as her chickens came home to roost with a vengeance. 'His father?' she repeated, stalling for time.

'He does have one?'

'Of course he has a father.' She knew

she couldn't keep up the pretence indefinitely, wouldn't have to since Faye and Kevin would be back in a day or two. She hated lying to him, by omission if nothing else, and was sorely tempted to tell him the truth and throw herself on his mercy. It hadn't worked with Dorothy Ashton and the Taplow Towers Residents' Association, but she suspected they had already been having second thoughts about letting her within their hallowed portals. She'd made an effort to look as middle-aged as possible for the interview, but she'd kept forgetting. They had probably been glad of the excuse . . .

'Patrick — '

'If he were mine, I'd want to know,' he said, not letting her speak. 'I wouldn't let him out of my sight.' His words were heartfelt and there was a darkly haunted look about his eyes that made her think again. There were buried passions here. Did he have a son of his own? A wife who made access difficult? Left the dog, taken the child.

He didn't linger to exchange confidences, but picked up the box. 'I'll take this upstairs,' he said abruptly.

'Thank you.' And she turned away, picked up Bertie's bottle to test the temperature. Then, as he sucked hungrily on it, it occurred to her that Learned Counsel must be hungry, too. 'Can I make you a sandwich, or something?' she offered. The unspoken 'before you go' once more hung between them in the air.

5

Patrick hesitated for a long moment, then he nodded and said, 'Thank you. That would be kind.' Jessie heard the slight edge in his voice, a suggestion that he knew she didn't mean to be. Which wasn't entirely true, but maybe it was wiser to let him think that.

'It's no trouble. I'll be making something for myself,' she assured him. She didn't want him thinking she was going out of her way to make him feel at home. 'Anything in particular?'

Patrick immediately regretted his sharpness. He didn't know her situation. He had no right to judge her. She might be in his house, but she hadn't set out to make his life difficult; he had Carenza to thank for that. He lifted his shoulders in the barest suggestion of a shrug. 'Anything but sieved fish or minced chicken,' he offered.

Jessie stared at him for a moment. Was that sarcasm? There was the slightest deepening of the laughter lines around his eyes, the faintest lift to the corners of his mouth. Had he made a joke?

Before she could get her head around it, show her appreciation with a smile, he was halfway upstairs.

It was probably as well, she thought irritably, concentrating on changing Bertie and trying hard to put Patrick Dalton and his deeply disturbing gold-grey eyes right out of her mind. She had plenty to keep her occupied. A long list of phone calls to make for a start; potential clients wouldn't stay on hold for long.

And now she'd committed herself to making her reluctant landlord some lunch. Would she never learn to keep her mouth shut?

She made a pile of cheese sandwiches, put a couple on a plate for herself, covered the rest and, with Bertie propped on her hip, she went upstairs.

'Mr Dalton?' He'd asked her to call him Patrick, but she had the feeling that things would be simpler if they kept things formal. The way he'd held her when she'd been scared by the dog, the way she'd felt when he'd held her, had left her in no doubt just how complicated it could get. And when had he discovered that kissing was a kinder cure than slapping for hysteria? Not that she was complaining. She'd take the kiss any time, if he was doing the kissing . . .

Which was why it was so complicated.

He'd left her box in the study rather than the box-room, but there was no sign of him. She put down her plate and went in search of him. 'Mr Dalton?' she called. 'Your sandwiches are in the . . . ' She stopped in the bedroom doorway. Patrick Dalton QC was stretched out on her bed. Or was that his bed? Wasn't possession nine-tenths of the law? If it was, he'd got it, because he was flat on his back and apparently fast asleep. 'Kitchen,' she finished, with a sigh.

She put Bertie into his cot, turned on

his little music box that played the Brahms lullaby, and stood beside him, stroking his cheek, trying to ignore the man lying on the bed behind her. Poor baby. Maybe, now his tooth was through, he'd be less fretful.

She smoothed the cover over him and turned reluctantly from the baby to the sleeping man. Despite her determination to get him out of her life, she couldn't be angry. He had to be close to exhaustion, which was something she could sympathise with. The urge to lie down beside him and have a nap herself was hard to resist.

But was it the bed, or the man in it that was so tempting? For someone who had forsworn the treachery of men, who knew how little a kiss meant, the decision should have been a piece of cake. Instead, the sudden eruption of suppressed feelings he'd brought boiling to the surface had turned what should have been a finger-click decision, something that needed no thought at all, into a multi-choice question.

Smothering a yawn, ignoring the pull of the bed — or the man in it — she decided to take the easy option and pass, and, turning away, she tiptoed towards the door.

Bertie wasn't having any of it. The minute she moved out of his line of sight, he began to whimper miserably.

'Shh,' she whispered. 'Let the poor man sleep.' The noise intensified. Damn! If Patrick had warned her he was going to take a nap, she'd have moved the cot into the study. But then, he probably hadn't intended to go to sleep. If he had he wouldn't have said yes to the sandwich. He'd have taken off more than his shoes and got under the covers.

There was a pack of painkillers beside the bed, presumably given to him at the hospital. Maybe he'd taken a couple and they'd knocked him out. With a combination of jet lag and the kind of twenty-four hours he'd had, it wouldn't take much. He'd probably sleep the clock round.

She lowered herself gently onto the

edge of the bed and restarted the lullaby. After the kind of two days she'd had, round the clock sounded wonderful, and she was forced to smother another huge yawn as the hypnotic little tune began to get to her.

She jumped up. She didn't have time to sleep; she had work to do. Bertie immediately began to whine. She hovered uncertainly between cot and door.

'Jessie, if you'd just sit down where he can see you he'd go to sleep.'

She swung round. Patrick didn't look any different. His eyes were still closed and he hadn't moved. 'I thought you were asleep.'

'So did I.' The first notes of the lullaby had drilled into his brain like a jackhammer. 'The combination of the music box, the baby and you jumping up and down like a jack-in-box persuaded me otherwise.'

'I'm sorry. I'll move the cot — '

He half raised lids that seemed to have weights attached to them. Jessie looked exhausted which, considering the night she'd had, was not surprising. 'You will not move the cot,' he said firmly. 'You will lie down and keep very still for a full ten minutes, by which time both Bertie and I will be fast asleep.' With any luck she would be too. 'At which point you can rush off and do whatever it is that's so desperately important.'

'You don't understand . . . '

No financial support, he thought. She's on her own and that's about as tough as it gets. But she still needed to rest. 'Ten minutes won't make much difference. And if it means Bertie settles more quickly?' He left her to choose the sensible option. She didn't let him down.

'You're probably right.'

'I'm always right,' he said as she lowered herself uncertainly to the bed with Bertie, his unwitting collaborator, watching every move, ready to let rip the moment she disappeared. 'Shoes off, feet up. That child is bright as a button; you won't fool him with half measures.'

'Mr Dalton — '

'Patrick.' He kept his eyes firmly fixed on the ceiling. 'We should be on first name terms if we're going to share a bed, don't you think, Jessie?'

'We're not sharing a bed!' He just patted the space beside him. 'Patrick, I don't think this is — '

'Don't. Think. At least not out loud. Just lie down and be very quiet. Please.' And he closed his eyes to reassure her, although sleep, which had overcome him so swiftly, so unexpectedly, would now have to be fought for, the darkness reclaimed inch by inch as it had been every night for ten years.

Feeling guilty for having disturbed him, and rather foolish for worrying about lying beside a man whose only desire was for sleep, Jessie kicked off her shoes and stretched out beside him, not quite touching, but still deeply conscious of the warmth of firm, muscular flesh a fingertip away, the scent of his skin mingling with freshly laundered sheets.

The lullaby was slowly winding

down, Bertie quietly cooing his own little pre-sleep song. It wouldn't take ten minutes. Five would be more than enough and then she'd creep out and leave the pair of them to it. She relaxed into the comfort of lavender-scented linen and closed her eyes.

Patrick, lying quietly beside her, listening for her breathing to shift into the soft rhythm of sleep, smiled. It became easier with practice, he discovered.

* * *

He stirred, opened bleary eyes, tried to recollect where he was, sift the dream from the reality. There was no urgency about it. He was warm and comfortable and he nestled back against the warm comfort of a woman's breast . . .

A woman's breast.

Even through the mind-deadening fug of the pain-killers he'd swallowed, he knew that was wrong. There was no comfort. Not here, not anywhere.

But the breast against which his head rested was as soft and sweet as any that haunted his dreams. And a lot warmer.

He should move, sort fact from fantasy, but, in truth, he'd much rather stay where he was. He brushed away the hair that was tangling with his lashes, real hair that felt like silk against his fingers. He struggled to get his woozy brain into a higher gear. No dream was that real, surely? And this time when he opened his eyes, they stayed open.

Jessie.

She didn't look much like a dream, but her shapeless T-shirt and baggy trousers didn't fool him for a minute. He knew what they concealed. And her face fell naturally into a smile. She had to work very hard to look cross, even when she was absolutely furious. Even asleep her lips parted slightly to reveal just a hint of teeth so that she looked as if she were inviting his kiss.

In that moment he knew exactly how the prince had felt when he'd found

Sleeping Beauty. And for a moment, a heartbeat, he succumbed to temptation, his mouth brushing against the softness of her lips. If he believed in magic, in fairy tales, he was the one who would wake from a curse . . . The promise had been there ever since he'd tugged at her ankle and been confronted, up close, by a pair of startled sea-coloured eyes.

He thought he'd had trouble when he'd walked into the bathroom and had discovered her asleep in the bath.

That hadn't been trouble, he realised as Jessie stirred, moved her head, nestled closer. Then she, too, seemed to realise that not everything was as it should be and she stilled, her eyes flickering open, not fully awake, but nearly there. *This* was trouble.

For a moment nothing happened as, in the dim light, she short-sightedly sifted the image she was seeing from what she had expected to see, a small frown puckering the space between her eyes. 'Graeme?' she murmured sleepily.

Graeme? Jealousy, as fierce as it was

unexpected, stabbed through him. 'Who's Graeme?' he asked, the words tumbling out before he could stop them.

'What?' She blinked, still on the outskirts of sleep.

'Is he Bertie's father?'

Jessie felt ghastly. Sleeping in the day fugged her brain, left her feeling fit for nothing . . . Then realisation hit her like a blast of smelling salts, clearing her head and leaving her in no doubt where she was and who she was sharing a bed with and she groaned. 'Oh, no. I don't believe it. I went to sleep.'

'You needed it.'

And not just beside him; she'd apparently thrown herself into Patrick Dalton's arms. It was getting to be a habit. First on the kitchen floor, then because of the dog . . . What on earth could she say? What on earth must he be thinking?

'We really must stop meeting like this,' she said. She needed to move. Really needed to move. She instructed her brain, but maybe it was still asleep because nothing happened. 'I should get up,' she said, just to prove that she meant it.

'Don't worry, Bertie's still asleep.'

Don't worry . . . 'Don't worry!' she repeated. Then stopped. Taking things logically, she knew he was right. There was nothing to worry about.

They were both fully dressed. Nothing had happened. They'd just rolled together the way people do . . .

Logic, she suspected, would always have trouble competing with a full-frontal embrace from a man like Patrick Dalton. Tall, with the kind of good looks that a man grows into, with the lines that only experience and maturity bring to a face.

Up close, in the daylight filtering in from the hall, she could see that there was already the faintest dusting of silver at his temples, could fully appreciate the aquiline nose, the kind of bone structure that the camera loved. Looks that only improve with age. She didn't doubt that he was the heartthrob of the central criminal court. Which was

152

presumably why his wife had cut her losses and quickly moved on — it was just a pity she hadn't taken her dog with her.

'Who's Graeme?' he repeated.

'What?' She didn't want to talk about him. 'Nobody. A man I lived with for a while . . . I must get up,' she said. His arm was draped over her thigh and he moved it slightly, tightened his hold. 'Really,' she said, meaning to sound firm, but missing it by a mile.

'You should take every chance you get to sleep, Jessie. When you have a baby to care for, work has to be put on the back burner.'

'Easy for you to say. I have to earn my own living.'

'I see.' Graeme was the kind of nobody who didn't contribute towards his son's upkeep, then. Or hers. Which made him feel considerably happier, even if it was tough on her.

'I very much doubt it. But you're right, I did need a nap. But now — ' Now her face was pressed against his throat. She could feel his pulse against her cheek, the faint prickle of his jaw against her forehead, the heavy, sensuous weight of his arm against her hips, holding her there, beside him. The temptation was to forget work, close her eyes and stay where she was . . .

He had a small scar, she noticed. On his chin. It was very old. Kevin had one just like it that he'd got playing rugby at school. Did Patrick play too?

Had he drifted off again? His eyes were closed. Maybe she shouldn't disturb him, but just lie there quietly until Bertie woke, maybe snatch a few more minutes herself . . .

But it was hard to sleep when, in her brain, the synapses were working overtime, sparking memories, jump starting hormones kept on a short leash for too long, stirring longings that she'd buried deep. Bertie, sweet Bertie, rescued her with a wail.

'It was too good to last.' Patrick moved his arm, let her go, watching her as she pulled down the rumpled T-shirt, picked up her precious baby. Graeme's baby. How could he not care . . . ? 'Do you know you've got baby food in your hair?' he said.

'Oh, thanks a bunch. I really needed to know that.'

'Any time,' he said, swinging himself off the bed. Maybe some fresh air and exercise would clear his head, get his brain working with its normal efficiency. One thing was for certain: if he stayed where he was, the only thing that would be working efficiently would have nothing to do with his mind. 'I'm going to take Grady out,' he said from the doorway. 'Are you cooking this evening, or shall I bring something back?'

'Cooking?' He'd meant for herself, had meant, Shall I bring something back for you? But she'd clearly misunderstood him because her face, which moments before had simply been distracted, was riven with a frown and it occurred to him that there was more than one way to shift an unwanted tenant. And the sooner she went the better. For both of them.

'Isn't that the reason most men prefer to share with women? They're domesticated. At home in the kitchen,' he added, just to really wind her up.

'Then you'll have to find a woman who can cook. And hope she'll invite you to dinner,' she yelled after him as he headed for the stairs. Bertie decided to join in.

'Well, boy,' he said as Grady leapt up and joyfully bounded after him as he headed through the garden to the garage, 'that was easy.' So why didn't he feel happier?

★   ★   ★

Jessie splashed her face with cold water, then stared at her reflection. He was just like Graeme. A user. He couldn't shift her, so he'd make the best of it.

The mirror revealed that, as well as the baby goo, set like concrete in her hair, there was a smear of rusk down her T-shirt. There was not so much as a trace of lipstick to improve things. Not that her mouth needed it. It looked full and hot, as if begging to be kissed. As if it had been kissed . . . She could still feel his breath against her cheek and she touched her lips with the tips of her fingers, as if she might feel some fleeting impression left by his mouth.

She let her hand fall. Who did she think she was? Sleeping Beauty? Even if she had been, he wouldn't have kissed her. He was a lawyer. He wouldn't be that stupid. Twice. Would he?

A traitorous part of her rather hoped he would.

Which was why she needed a breathing space before she saw him again, and, instead of going downstairs, she crossed the landing to the study and turned on her cellphone.

It was almost a relief to discover that there were a load of messages demanding her immediate attention. She put Bertie down on the floor and, while he chewed happily on her trouser leg, she returned calls and made promises that she hoped she could keep. Then she called Kevin and Faye.

'I hope you're having a wonderful time,' she said, when invited to leave a message. 'Someone should be. By the way, Bertie's got a tooth.'

* * *

'A tooth! He's got his first tooth and I wasn't there!' Faye clung to Kevin, sobbing into his shoulder.

'Shh. Don't fret, sweetheart, he'll have lots more teeth.'

'But not a first one!'

'I know, but . . . um . . . this was your idea. Remember?'

'I remember. And I suppose it's worth it, if it gets Jessie out of that awful flat.' Faye sniffed. 'She sounded really fed up, didn't she?'

'Well, that's a good sign.'

'Is it?'

'Would you be happy if you'd just been thrown out of your home?'

★ ★ ★

Phone calls made, Jessie turned her mind to dinner. Mr Dalton wanted domesticity, did he? To come home from his run to a shower and the little woman slaving away over a hot stove?

Fat chance. She never could get a cake to rise, or potatoes to crisp — at least not in time to coincide with anything else she was cooking. And even if she had been the next best thing to a cordon bleu cook, he wouldn't be treated to a demonstration of her talents. The more uncomfortable he was, the quicker he'd realise there was nothing to be gained by hanging around.

Nothing.

She glanced at the crumpled bed, straightened it.

No more cosy naps for two for a start.

She rinsed the goo out of her hair. He'd be expecting a hot shower when he returned which, under the terms of her lease, she was paying for. She turned off the water heater.

Then she changed her T-shirt, loaded the washing machine — she was losing count of how many times she'd done that since Bertie entered her life — and checked out the cupboards in the kitchen.

Baked beans, breakfast cereals, a packet of lentils. The freezer yielded nothing more exciting than a package of nut cutlets. There was one left. If Patrick wanted to stay for supper he'd have to choose between staying at home and entertaining Bertie, or visiting the nearest supermarket.

They could tackle the vexed question of who would do the cooking once they had some groceries to cook.

* * *

Patrick discovered that attempting to run was over-ambitious. And how long could a man run from what haunted him?

He tossed a stick for Grady, walking slowly across the park, trying to make sense out of the turmoil of conflicting emotions that had been waging a war inside him ever since he'd encountered the disturbing Jessica Hayes.

He'd told Molly that he hadn't been interested in a new relationship since Bella had died. The truth was more complex. Initially he'd been too numb to respond to even the most blatant offers of comfort. In the wake of the numbness came ice, a cold force field that repelled even the most flirtatious female.

Arriving home in the middle of the night with nothing more on his mind than how long it would take Carenza to pack, though, his defences had been down and he'd been vulnerable.

Which explained his shockingly immediate and vital response to the burglar-berating Amazon who'd taken up residence in his house.

Maybe.

Most men, unexpectedly confronted with a beautiful woman — especially after seeing her naked in the bath — would respond in that way. It didn't mean anything. Or it wouldn't, except that the desire wasn't going away. Her smile was like the sun heating him up. Her scowl made him want to hold her, kiss away the frown. And when she was angry . . . well, it was better that he didn't dwell on what that did to him.

Which might just have been rather wonderful, but for the baby. The baby was complicating things. They were such a neat little package. It was too obvious; there was too dangerous a temptation to grab it with both hands. Bella and his baby daughter, Mary Louise, were dead. Jessica and Bertie fitted the gaping hole in his life like a cork fitted a bottle.

It was rather like love on the rebound. In his case the spring had been straining for ten years, which probably explained why the kickback was so fierce, his reaction so intense.

*   *   *

The washing machine was busy, but otherwise the kitchen was empty when he got back. He gave Grady a drink then, shutting the dog outside, he went upstairs. Jessica was curled up on the sofa, making notes. She made no sign that she was conscious of his presence. Well, what had he expected? Arms around his neck, a joyous, 'Darling, you're home'?

'Are you aware that your infant is dribbling on a valuable carpet?' he demanded tetchily. 'And that your cat is leaving hair all over the upholstery?'

She looked up, peering over the top of her spectacles. 'Mao is not my cat. I don't like cats. I would never willingly live with one.' Then, she added, 'But, given the choice between a cat and a man, I'll take the cat.'

'About the same way I feel about you, then,' Patrick said. And hoped he sounded convincing. Once they'd gone — and they would go, soon — he'd get the place cleaned from attic to base-ment. Get rid of the warm baby smell that was tearing him to shreds. Get rid of the mind-changing scent of Jessica

Hayes before it invaded his very soul. Get back to normal. 'Make sure you clean the carpet before you leave.'

She glanced at it, but didn't move. 'If it's that valuable it should be done professionally. In fact when I cleaned up some chocolate — '

'Chocolate?'

' — I noticed several other marks. There's one there . . . ' and she nodded ' . . . right by your foot. Red wine, at a guess.'

'I'll take your word for it. And your advice. Just tell me where to send the bill.'

'You're not going to be one of *those* landlords, are you, Patrick?'

His name on her lips sounded so perfect . . . 'I'm not going to be any kind of landlord,' he said abruptly. Then, because he couldn't help himself, 'What kind?'

'The kind of landlord that makes up all kinds of excuses not to give back the deposit at the end of a tenancy.'

'You didn't give me a deposit.'

'The kind of landlord that I would take to the small claims court without a second thought.'

'Very funny.' But, having reinforced his determination that she should leave — at least, he thought he'd reinforced his determination — he changed the subject. 'Busy? Making a list of letting agencies to call?' he asked hopefully.

'No,' she said, tapping a pencil against her teeth. 'I'm making a shopping list. The cupboard, as they say, is bare.'

'Is it? Well, enjoy yourself amongst the loaves and spinach, I'm going to take a shower.'

Jessie pushed her spectacles down her nose and looked up at him. The damp strands of his hair were clinging wetly to his forehead and neck and he looked rather pale. 'Are you all right?' she asked, anxiety clutching at her heart. Then, more briskly, 'I don't think you should be running so soon after that crack on the head.'

'I'm touched by your concern, but Grady did most of the running.'

'I'm glad to hear it.' Then, feeling horribly guilty at draining the hot water tank, she said, 'I'm afraid the water might not be very hot; I've had the washing machine running. It's going non-stop when you've got a baby.'

He shrugged. 'The heater's on . . . Isn't it?'

'I'm afraid not. Just for an hour in the morning and an hour in the evening while I'm paying the bill.'

He took a deep breath. 'Don't worry about the bill; I'll pay it. Just leave the heater on in future.'

Damn, damn, damn, she cursed silently. How could she have been so mean? 'Can I have that in writing?'

'I'll see to it.'

'Thanks.' He was going to be hard to shift. But she couldn't risk having him around. He was too potent a reminder of what she'd given up. She was going to have to be tough. 'I'll leave the list on the kitchen table, shall I?' she enquired, pushing him further.

'List?'

'If you want to eat, you'll have to do the shopping. I have to feed Bertie and then it'll be bathtime and I'll have to put him to bed.'

There was a pause as he appeared to gather himself. 'You don't eat, I take it?'

'When I said the cupboard was bare, I was thinking of you. I've got a tin of baked beans for my supper. And a nut cutlet,' she added recklessly.

'Just the one?'

Jessie regarded Patrick thoughtfully. Had he ever seen the inside of a supermarket? she wondered. He must have someone who looked after him, or at least his house. A 'treasure' to clean and shop, although she doubted that he cooked much. Good-looking, unattached men were always in demand for dinner parties. Always in demand, full stop. She was certain that if he tried, he could find someone to take him in.

And if he called her bluff? Went shopping?

She shrugged. She'd worry about that in the unlikely event that it happened. 'Just the one. Of course, you're welcome to share it.'

'Thank you, Jessica. That's very kind.'

She hated to be called Jessica, a fact she was fairly certain he'd worked out for himself, but she matched his impressive self-control. She'd hoped he'd go out. Move out. At the very least lose his temper and tell her to go to the devil so that she'd know she was getting to him.

Now she was faced with the prospect of cooking that unappetising-looking cutlet and sharing it with him. Or backing down. She should have stopped while she was ahead, with the baked beans.

6

Patrick stood beneath the icy blast of the shower and promised she'd pay for putting him through this. In nut cutlets if that was what it took. Not that he'd believed in her nut-cutlet-for-one any more than he'd believed that she'd used all the hot water washing baby clothes.

Water this cold could only have been caused by someone leaving a tap on until all the hot water had been drained from the tank.

Extravagant, indeed!

Very well, if she wanted a fight she could have it. No doubt she believed she was winning easily, he thought, roughly towelling the warmth back into his skin. She was mistaken. He might have taken one fall and come close to a knockout when he'd woken with her in his arms earlier on, but there was no way he was going to submit.

He'd share whatever meagre fare she chose to produce for supper, happy in the knowledge that she was suffering too.

As he passed the study, he glanced through the open door. She was sitting at her computer and, interested to see what his tenant did for a living, he went to investigate. But she wasn't working; she was catching up on her lunch as she surfed the net.

'Good, are they?' he asked as she took a bite from a sandwich.

'A bit dried up. I made some for you. They're in the kitchen.'

'Thanks. What are you looking for?'

'Somewhere to live.' She clicked the mouse and the screen went dark. 'I was signing on with some estate agents.'

'You've decided to look for somewhere else to rent?' He managed to keep the relief out of his voice. It was disturbingly easy.

'No, I've had enough of difficult landlords.' She smiled as she gathered Bertie and headed for the stairs. He ignored her obvious attempt at provocation, instead noting that she'd used the plural. Which begged the question, why had she moved so precipitately from her previous accommodation? The lease she'd signed still lay on the hall table and he picked it up as he followed her down into the kitchen. 'I've decided it's time to bite the bullet and buy a place of my own. Apparently I can just about afford a broom cupboard — '

'Buy?' he repeated, distracted from his train of thought. 'But that'll take months.'

'Will it?' She glanced at the lease he was holding. '*More* than three months, do you think?'

'Probably,' he said, recognising the challenge. 'Unless you find something straight away. Is your lease renewable?'

She grinned. 'No. Carenza was very firm about that. Now I know why. Can you wait for your supper? I have to feed Bertie.' If he was hungry, he might go out.

'I think I can manage to contain my

excitement. I dare say the sandwiches will keep me going.'

'Good,' Jessie said, deeply regretting her lack of foresight in not flinging them out for the birds while she had a chance. She must have been mad offering to make them. Impulsive. It was a hard habit to break.

She needn't have worried. The plate which had contained the sandwiches was in several pieces on the kitchen floor. There was no sign of bread or cheese. Only Grady, stretched across the step wearing the expression of a dog who knows he's been very bad, and Jessie found herself in the unexpected situation of wanting to hug him.

'Oh, dear,' she said as Patrick shut the door, releasing her from the safety of the hallway. 'I'm afraid that was the last of the cheese. And you broke the eggs last night. I'm not usually this badly organised. It was moving — '

'Unexpectedly. I know. But I did shut Grady outside.'

'I promise you, I didn't let him in.'

'No.' Patrick knew she wouldn't have done that. 'Maybe I didn't shut the door properly.'

'Maybe Grady is smarter than you think.'

'He's obedient,' he said, 'and he'll roll over and die for the Queen with the best of them. But open a door? I think not.' He held out his hand. 'You'd better give me the list.'

'List?'

'The shopping list. That was the plan. I shop, you cook.'

'You don't fancy the nut cutlet, then?' She clearly didn't expect an answer because she tore the sheet out of her notebook and handed it to him.

A quick glance informed him that it contained the kind of food that gave vegetarianism a bad name. 'This is everything you want?' he enquired, looking up. 'No nuts?'

'Oh, gosh, thanks for reminding me,' she said brightly, ignoring the sarcasm in his voice. 'And since you're going . . . ' She retrieved the list, added half a dozen items, then handed it back. 'I'd better give you some money,' she said, looking around for her hand-bag.

'Don't bother.' She didn't look that happy, Patrick noticed, considering she'd got her own way. Did she imagine he considered himself above pushing a trolley around a supermarket? Or was there some other reason her conscience was bothering her? Clinging to her doubtful lease, for instance? Or was it something rather more basic? He picked up a baby-food jar, washed and ready for the recycling bin, and found the label highly informative. 'You can settle up later.'

'Right. Thanks.'

'Cheer up, at least you won't have to share your precious nut cutlet.'

She relaxed, smiled. 'I wouldn't have minded.'

'You're a saint.' His words didn't sound terribly sincere, but then he hadn't meant them to. 'Tell me, have you been a vegetarian long?'

'What?' She flushed with confusion.

'Oh, well . . . um . . . I started when I was fifteen . . . '

'Really? I wondered if it might have been a spur-of-the-moment decision. Since you were feeding Bertie *lamb* and carrot hotpot for his lunch.' He turned the jar so that she could see the label. Then, taking her free hand in his, he placed it in her palm. 'I offer you exhibit . . . ' About to say A, he remembered the cricket bat. 'Exhibit B.'

He didn't give her a chance to answer but left her standing there, in the middle of the kitchen, with her mouth open. Which would teach her to be economical with the truth.

★ ★ ★

Jessie knew that saying the first thing that popped into her head was not very bright. She must be cracking up under the strain, she decided as she replaced the jar on the draining board. Her brain was turning to baby mush.

There was no other excuse for the

way she'd been behaving. She didn't have to play stupid games. She had rights. She had a lease signed by his niece acting in his absence. All complaints should be addressed to Carenza Finch and when Patrick came back she would tell him that. Quietly but firmly. Explain that he'd have to make alternative living arrangements for the next three months.

He was an intelligent man. He might not like it, but he must see that she was right.

Then she sighed. It sounded fine in theory, but in practice she knew he wouldn't see anything of the sort. And why should he? This was his house and he had every right to expect to be able to occupy it without let or hindrance. Niece notwithstanding.

She groaned, sat down and laid her forehead on the kitchen table. She worked hard, paid her taxes, and in return all she asked for was a quiet life. What on earth had she done to deserve this?

★ ★ ★

Patrick headed straight for the meat counter. A big fat steak should do it, he thought, flamed beneath the grill and served very rare. If she really was a vegetarian — and it was a big 'if' — it would revolt her. If she wasn't, she could watch him eat it while she played with her nut cutlet and suffer.

Either way would be just fine with him.

It wasn't nice, but neither was her attempt to bring him to his knees with beans and bran.

It was just as well she didn't know how close his knees were to the floor already.

He tossed the meat into the trolley and, in case that didn't do it, he stocked up with thick sausages and middle-cut bacon for breakfast, although the thought of actually eating them made him feel slightly queasy.

The doctor in the emergency room hadn't bothered to tell him to take it easy; the presence of the police had doubtless given him the impression that his patient would be locked up and enduring enforced idleness for the foreseeable future. He, on the other hand, had anticipated a day in bed, recovering quietly. On his own.

By any standards, for a man who'd had a crack on the head, he'd been overdoing it.

He took a couple of deep breaths, then sought out the rice and beans and the organically produced eggs, carrots and onions Jessica had stipulated on her list. Her last-minute additions included a couple of things for Bertie. Powder, wipes.

The queasiness intensified.

He was staring blindly at the shelves, lost in memories, when a woman with an infant strapped into her trolley stopped and asked if he'd pass her a pack of nappies from the top shelf. Dragged back from the past, he reached for the pack and passed it to her.

'Do you need some help?' she said as she stowed it in her trolley.

'Help?'

'You look a bit lost.' She didn't wait for him to confirm or deny it. 'New arrival, is it? I think it's so nice when a man gets really involved.' She took the list from him. 'What did you have?' she asked as she picked out the things Jessica had listed.

A daughter. Mary Louise. He'd been there and had put his newborn daughter into Bella's arms . . . 'This is for Bertie,' he said quickly.

'Bertie? How sweet. What's it short for?' His mind groped for an answer. 'Albert? Robert?' She rattled on, oblivious to his blank expression.

'It's just Bertie,' he said quickly, when an expectant silence warned him that it was his turn to speak.

'Well, you take care of them both. It's tough doing it all on your own. I know.'

'Yes, I suppose it is. Thanks for your help.' He turned back to the bright little baby toys. They didn't change, he thought. Just the colours. He took one down and held it for a moment, then tossed it in with the rest of the shopping.

It was a mistake. He realised that when he reached the checkout.

He picked the bright little toy out of the trolley and held it for a moment. He'd come out intent on a little payback. Now, as the steak and sausages and bacon travelled down the conveyer towards the cashier, he felt less than heroic.

He'd always seen himself as a champion of the underdog, willing to go into bat for lost causes and sometimes winning against all the odds. If Jessie Hayes had been his client he would be making damn sure no one kicked her out of a house she had rented in good faith. She shouldn't have to suffer because his niece had a very poor grasp of the verities.

Who could say what she'd been through? And, selfishly, he was doing his utmost to make things worse just to save himself from the mental pins and needles as long-numbed emotions were unexpectedly cranked into action.

Maybe, he thought, they could start

again. Come to some sensible arrangement. It shouldn't be beyond the wit of two civilised adults to share a house for a few days while she found somewhere else. It just needed a little give and take. And if he was giving more than she knew . . . well, that was his business.

'Do you want that?' the girl at the checkout asked him.

'What? Oh, yes. Sorry.' He put it down on the conveyer and reached for his wallet, then carried everything to the car.

He didn't immediately head for home. If she was going to stay, he wanted it to be on his terms, not hers.

At the letting agency a middle-aged woman with a professional smile waved him to a chair. 'Good afternoon, sir. How can I help you?'

'I need to speak to whoever arranged the lease on twenty-seven Cotswold Street.' The woman frowned. 'You let it to a Miss Jessica Hayes earlier this week,' he prompted.

'I remember Miss Hayes. She phoned

in a terrible state. Sarah tried to help, but she needed something immediately and we can't take short cuts with references.'

'Someone did.'

'Not us.' She shook her head. 'Besides, we don't have any properties in Cotswold Road. I only wish we had.'

'Then maybe you'd better ask Sarah to explain this.'

'Sarah isn't working here any more,' she said, taking the lease from him. 'She was just temping, making some money to go backpacking in Europe. I can't see the attraction myself — ' Then, as she scanned the document he'd handed her, the smile finally slipped and she uttered a very unprofessional word.

★ ★ ★

Jessie decided to be grown up and own up.

She didn't eat a lot of meat, but she wasn't a vegetarian. Not that she'd lied about becoming one when she was fifteen; she just hadn't mentioned that she'd lost interest three days later, when she'd been invited to a barbecue by a boy she'd been making eyes at for months.

It wasn't a bit like her and she'd make up for her lapse in good manners by ordering something for them both from her favourite Italian restaurant and having it delivered. Chicken with soft polenta and game chips, she thought. Followed by zabaglione and ratafia biscuits. Maybe even a bottle of something. That would make a suitable peace offering.

She didn't give herself a chance to get cold feet, but called the restaurant straight away.

She'd just finished giving her order, confirming delivery for seven-thirty, when she heard the click of the door handle and felt a rush of cool air as it was opened behind her.

'Gosh, you were quick,' she said, fixing a bright smile to her lips even as she mentally kicked herself for dallying when she could have been making a bit of an effort with her appearance. Removing the lingering traces of baby food might have impressed Patrick with her credentials as a woman who was in charge of her life, a woman who wasn't going to take any nonsense from him, just because he was a big, scary lawyer.

But it wasn't Patrick. It was Grady standing on the doorstep, with that soppy look dogs wore when they wanted to play.

That was bad.

But it was going to get worse.

Mao, picking fussily at the remains of the fish, looked up as the door opened; looked up and froze.

For a moment nothing happened.

Then Grady lowered his huge shaggy head and sniffed curiously at the cat.

★ ★ ★

Poor Jessie. She'd clung to her lease like a lifeline and it wasn't worth the paper it was written on. One of Carenza's friends had bypassed the formalities, after running off a copy of the standard lease.

She didn't know. He'd bank on it. Which put him at an unfair advantage. Maybe he should forget the steak, order some decent food for supper so that neither of them had to cook. It had, after all, been a trying day for both of them.

Chinese or Indian would be best, he thought, if it was going to be vegetarian. With a little goodwill and a decent wine to help things along, they should be able to sort things out. On his terms. She could have the boxroom. And the study.

He grinned as he pulled into the garage and made a call to a nearby restaurant from his car phone before heading through the garden with the groceries.

The kitchen door was standing open and Grady was nowhere to be seen.

He dropped the bags, careless of the organically produced eggs he'd sought out on Jessie's carefully listed instructions. He didn't have time to worry about a few cracked eggs, or about the scattered remains of the precious china that had, when he'd left the house, decorated the Welsh dresser on the far wall of the kitchen.

Worry wasn't a word he'd use. The sight of the overturned high chair, the spatter of blood on the kitchen floor didn't worry him. He felt fear. Deep, desperate fear. 'Jessie?' he yelled, running even as the bags hit the floor, chasing the trail of destruction. 'Jessie, where are you?'

The front hall had been wrecked. Pictures were askew, the table had been tipped over, the telephone ripped from its connection and cracked. A large weeping fig lay trampled and dying amidst a confusion of paw prints, small and large, in the scattered compost. It didn't take a forensic scientist to decipher the evidence.

'Jessie!' He hoped, prayed, to find her cowering in the drawing room. After a heart-stopping glance he saw that it was untouched. And empty. 'Jessie!' The fear was beginning to echo in his voice. If she'd run . . . Grady was gentle, but dogs were pack animals . . . 'Answer me, Jessie! Where the hell are you?'

The chaos continued up the stairs and he took them three at a time, pausing on the threshold of the bedroom. Grady was standing, four-square on the bed, teeth bared, hackles raised, his nose bearing the bloody scars of his encounter with the cat.

'Grady! Down!' The dog dropped like a stone to lie flat on the bed, head down, while the cat hissed derision from the safety of the curtain rail. Patrick flung open the bathroom door. 'Jessie!' There was no sign of her. It was a nightmare. He shouldn't have left her. Heart pounding, and with a firm grip on Grady's collar, he started back downstairs, flinging open doors as he went. He'd come to a halt in the hall, wondering if she might have run out of the front door and into the street, when he heard the muffled sound of someone calling his name. A distant thumping.

He stopped. Listened. It was coming from the kitchen. From the broom cupboard beneath the stairs.

He opened the door and Jessie, curled up in a foetal hunch and clutching Bertie to her breast, fell out of the cupboard in a tangle of brooms and mops. 'I thought you were never coming,' she gasped. 'Didn't you hear me shouting?'

Relief that she was unhurt, that they were both unhurt, was swamped by anger as dark as it was sudden.

'Hear you?' he echoed. 'Madam, do you think I would have been calling your name for the last five minutes — ' while his mind provided pictures of every imaginable nightmare ' — if I'd *heard* you?'

'I shouted as loud as I could,' she protested. She brushed some fluff from her face and sneezed. Then, eyeing Grady nervously, she asked, 'Is it bad?'

He gestured at the wreck of the kitchen. 'A bad-tempered elephant might have done worse,' he suggested, pushing Grady outside and shutting the door. 'I hope you can come up with some sufficiently convincing explanation for the insurance company.'

'Insurance company?' She stared at him. Was that all he was bothered about? The mess? A few old plates? 'You bet I'll have something convincing to tell the insurance company,' she began angrily, before catching her breath on a shuddering sob. 'Oh, damn!' she said, clutching Bertie close, dropping tender kisses on the soft downy little head. 'Damn your insurance company. And your plates. What on earth would I have done? Said? If anything bad had happened to Bertie?'

'Don't,' he said, reaching out awkwardly, not quite touching her. To touch her would be all it would take to dissolve the last of his defences, to betray the precious memories . . . 'Please, don't . . . '

'If anything had happened to Bertie because I was too stupid, too afraid . . . ' A tear squeezed out from beneath her shuttered lids and slid down her cheek. Then another.

'It didn't,' Patrick said, abandoning

caution, kneeling beside her and reaching for her, reaching for them both and this time taking them into his arms, holding them close. 'Nothing happened. Nothing will happen,' he said. 'It's all right.' He kissed Bertie's little head. 'Nothing but a little dust.' He kissed her curls.

She looked up, tears making rivulets in her dusty cheeks. 'I'm sorry.'

'No, I'm sorry.' He kissed her forehead. 'I didn't mean to shout but I was so scared . . . you can't know . . . ' He shuddered. 'I don't want you ever to know,' he said fiercely. She blinked. 'I should never have left you on your own when I knew you were scared. I . . . I'm just sorry. Please, Jessie, don't cry.'

Jessie rubbed at her cheek with the flat of her hand, then looked up into his face. 'You're crying, too,' she said, reaching up to touch his cheek as if she couldn't quite believe it. It was wet. 'Patrick, you're trembling.' And then somehow she was the one doing the comforting, holding him, her hand about his neck, her cheek against his. 'It's all right. Really. See?' She managed a smile. 'Nothing happened to us. And you're right, if I hadn't been frozen to the spot like a total wimp, none of this would have happened. It was my fault, not Grady's. Really.' She stroked his face, kissed his cheek. It was wet and salty and she held her cheek against his, wanting to reassure him, wanting him to know that she was safe, Bertie was safe. 'Here,' she said softly, her hand flat against his cheek so that he had to look at her, see that what she said was true. And when he looked at her she touched her lips to his.

For a moment they were quite still, not breathing. Then his mouth parted beneath her lips and he kissed her as if he was drawing the very breath from her body.

For ten years he'd been a dead man walking and now this woman, who'd taken over his house, was taking over his heart, bringing it pumping back to life, making it feel, making it hurt. It wasn't what he wanted. He wanted to be left alone with his memories. They were all he had and he was so afraid that if he didn't concentrate they'd slip away from him. Yet to hold Jessie, feel her skin beneath his hand, taste the very essence of her filling his mouth, was like an ache, a yearning, a desperate need. She was offering him the kiss of life . . .

'Jessie . . . don't, please . . . '

He pulled back, stood up before she could reach out for him. 'What on earth were you doing in the broom cupboard, anyway?' he said abruptly, distancing himself from her, from his feelings. There was too much emotion flying about for sense to prevail.

'What the hell do you think I was doing?' she demanded, left to struggle to her feet with Bertie because he didn't dare touch her and hurt, prickly at his abrupt change of manner. 'I was hiding from the Hound of the Baskervilles . . . '

'Grady isn't — ' He stopped. Arguing

about the dog's temperament would get them nowhere. He dragged his fingers through his hair. 'It didn't occur to you to just go into the hall and close the door behind you?'

'I didn't actually have a lot of time to weigh up the best course of action,' she replied loftily, trying to pretend that nothing had happened. Then she sneezed, somewhat spoiling the effect. He wanted to laugh. He controlled himself, a bit late in the day, but at least he was finally making the effort. 'The broom cupboard wouldn't have been my first choice, believe me. I just opened the first door that came to hand and dived in.' She sneezed again, groped in her pocket for a tissue. There wasn't one. He produced a handkerchief, offered it to her without comment. She grabbed it in time for the third sneeze. Then, eyes streaming, she said, 'Besides, your dog can open doors.'

'Don't talk rubbish.'

'Rubbish is it? Well, how do you think he got in?'

'Maybe the catch is loose . . . ' He

went to check it, glad to put some distance between them, gain some breathing space, but immediately wanting to be close again. He grasped the door handle and shook it. It held. He shrugged. 'It couldn't have been shut properly, but that's beside the point. None of this would have happened if your cat hadn't been here.'

'Mao is not my cat!'

'If you hadn't been here, then!'

'Wrong on both counts. None of this would have happened if *you* hadn't been here! If you had honoured a lease I entered into in good faith!'

'About that lease — ' he began, but she wasn't listening.

'I'd just finished a phone call and I'd picked up Bertie when I heard the d-d-door open.' Jessie was shaking again, but it wasn't all Grady's fault. She'd kissed him. Just kissed him. *Just!* What a joke. Except she felt like weeping. It wasn't *just*. It was nine point five on the Richter scale of kisses, earth-shattering, the kind of kiss that could change your life. And he'd stopped it. Pulled away. Stood up and walked away. Jessie's teeth began to judder as reaction set in and her legs buckled. 'I thought it was you and I turned round and . . . '

'Hey, steady.' Patrick caught her as her legs gave way. Caught her and held her, taking the baby before supporting her up the stairs to the drawing room. Once she was safely installed in a chair, he put Bertie down on the carpet — one dribble more or less would make no difference — and he poured a large measure of brandy into a glass. 'Here.' He held out the glass. Jessie pulled back at the smell but Patrick wasn't taking no for an answer this time. He hunkered down and held the glass to her lips. 'It's medicinal,' he said grimly. 'Drink it.'

She sipped, gagged, shuddered, but the heat of the spirit seemed to revive her. 'God, that's horrible.'

'The worse the taste, the better the medicine. Again.' He repeated the dose, with the same result. He just couldn't believe anyone could be so utterly ... dumb. So completely adorable. 'I didn't hear you, but you must have heard me calling out to you. Why didn't you come out when you knew I was home?' he asked.

'I couldn't. There wasn't a handle on the inside. I banged and shouted ... ' She shrugged.

'No handle?' He imagined her horror when she'd realised, and tried not to smile.

All he had to do was remember the way he'd felt, just how frantic he'd been, and he needed to take a medicinal sip of the brandy to steady his own frazzled nerves. Then, remembering how he'd felt when he'd held her, when she'd touched his cheek, when he'd kissed her, he drained the glass. 'I searched the whole damn house ... ' he began. Then he lifted his shoulders, an awkward admission that she was right. 'I was so scared you'd been hurt.'

'Were you? I thought I cornered the market in 'scared'.'

'Not a chance.' He put a hand over hers. 'Jessie, I'm sorry. Truly sorry that you had such a fright.'

And the kiss, Jessie wondered, was he sorry about that, too? Again? She sighed. 'So am I. Really sorry.' Quite which of her sins she was apologising for, she wasn't certain.

'No problem. Nothing that can't be fixed.' He obviously assumed she was talking about the destruction of his house, which was probably just as well. If he'd asked . . . 'Well, maybe not the china,' he said. 'I'd better go and clear it up.'

'I should do it. It was all my fault — '

'No!' Then, more gently, he said, 'None of this was your fault. Leave it to me.'

Downstairs in the kitchen, Patrick righted the high chair, then went to look for a box while Jessie, who had followed him downstairs despite his instructions to stay put, fastened Bertie into it. 'It'll be quicker with two,' she said when he turned round. Then, gathering up the larger pieces of china and handing them to him, she asked, 'Was this stuff very valuable?'

'Valuable?' Patrick was holding a plate that had survived the mayhem but for a chip on the rim, turning it over abstractedly, Jessie thought, as if seeking some kind of answer to her question. 'That rather depends on what you mean by valuable. I bought this for Bella at an antique fair just after we were married.'

'Your wife?' The one who'd left him with the dog for company, although any man who could kiss like Patrick Dalton seemed capable of making his own social arrangements.

'It was her birthday. She was twenty-six — ' which was more than she wanted to know, Jessie thought ' — and she saw this plate. We had dinner on the way home. I can't remember where. You think you'll never forget, but you do — '

'You're divorced?' she asked, anxious

to put a stop to his trip down memory lane, since it didn't seem to be making him happy. And, since he'd kissed her first, she was entitled to know.

'Divorced?' He looked distracted. 'Oh. No.'

Oh, great! 'Well,' she said, quickly, 'it's not too, too badly damaged. It wouldn't show if you stood it like this. See?' She spoke with forced brightness as she stood it on the dresser with the chipped edge behind the plate rail.

'No.' He reached over her shoulder. 'Chipped plates are good for nothing but keeping germs. Bella only collected perfect pieces.' He dropped the plate in the box.

Jessie blinked at the sudden savagery of it.

Collected. Past tense. She hadn't left him, Jessie realised, far too late. She might have left the dog, but she wouldn't have left her precious collection of plates. They weren't divorced. His wife was dead.

'Well,' she said uncertainly, 'if they

were all insured — '

'Insured?' Patrick stared into the box of broken china. 'What value could you put on the memory of a day spent together, Jessie? A moment that can never be repeated. Tell me where you can insure memories so that they're never lost, don't slip away from you or fade like an old sepia photograph.'

Jessie swallowed, wishing she'd done as she was told and stayed in the drawing room. But she was in too deep now; she'd stirred up too much pain to walk away. 'What happened to her?'

He turned then, stared at her, as if no one had ever dared to ask him that before. Ever dared speak of it. 'She was hit by a drunk driver. He was going so fast that, even if he'd seen the lights, he wouldn't have been able to stop.'

'Ten years ago?' He nodded. 'I'm so sorry.' She made a helpless gesture at the shattered china. She wanted to go to him, take his hand, put her arms around him, hold him as he'd held her. But there was a stiffness about him. A distance that couldn't be breached. 'I'm truly sorry.'

'In the scale of life's disasters, a few broken plates don't matter much, I suppose. A few broken memories — '

'Memories don't break, Patrick.' He looked up, frowned. 'Not if you want to keep them.' She picked up a piece that he'd missed. 'These are just props, like photographs. Potent reminders but, if the photograph gets lost, all you've really lost is a piece of paper. Memory is inside you, in your head, in your heart. The way you smile when you hear a tune you both loved, a flash of the colour she wore when you first met . . . Only the pain fades. If you let it. If you don't keep poking at it like a sore tooth. If you make new memories.' She handed him the fragment of china. 'It's why the sun is always shining in childhood summers. Why ice cream tasted better.'

Patrick took the piece of china she was holding, turned it over in his hands. It had been a ribbon plate. The first piece he'd ever bought for the lovely woman he'd married and, two short years later, buried with their baby beside her. 'Is that true?'

'I hope so.' He looked up then, and she saw the questions forming behind his eyes. 'I'd better put Bertie to bed,' she said quickly, fumbling with the straps. 'I was just going to when . . . well . . . ' She let it go. 'Will you be all right?'

'Yes, Jessie. I'll be fine.' He stood up, unfastened Bertie from the chair for her, holding him for a moment. 'He's a fine boy.'

'Yes. I just hope he doesn't give me as much trouble as Carenza gives you.'

'I'd echo that,' he said. 'But I comfort myself with the knowledge that I can summon her father as a last resort.' He handed the baby back to her, quickly turning away.

'Patrick, about dinner — '

'Don't worry about it,' he said.

'No — ' she began.

'Or moving out. Three months isn't

long. We'll sort something out.'

Months? He'd planned on a few days. A few weeks at the most. When had a few days become three months? Between his brain and his mouth? Between lunch and dinner? Between the past and the present?

His heart was pounding painfully as he picked up the box. He was sure the insurance company would want to see the evidence. Quite what their reaction would be ... He stopped, leaned against the door, shaking too much to move any further. He'd clung to his bitter memories for so long, used the pain and anger to drive himself from day to day. He'd been so afraid that if he let go he'd have nothing ...

'Patrick — '

'What?' He glared at Jessie and the child she was holding, hating the sympathy in her voice. She took a step back as if his anger was a physical thing.

'I ... you looked as if you might faint ... '

'I'm fine. I'm sorry, I didn't mean to

bark at you.' He wasn't angry with her. 'Put Bertie to bed and then we'll talk about how we can split the house between us.'

She hesitated, then said, 'I think you mean to be kind, Patrick. But we both know it won't work.'

7

'Won't work?' Patrick could scarcely believe his ears. 'What do you mean it won't work?'

'I might be able to share with you, Patrick, but I can't live with your dog.'

'*Might? Might* be able to share with me? Of all the ungrateful — ' He stopped himself. She had no reason to be grateful, she didn't know that the lease was a phoney. Grady was the problem here, not him. He put down the box and reached for the kitchen phone. The line was dead and he swore. 'Do you have your mobile handy?'

Her bag was on the kitchen table and she took out her phone and handed it to him without a word and watched while he punched in Molly's number. 'Molly?'

'Hello, Patrick. How're you getting on with your lovely lodger?'

'Do you want the short version or will you wait for the book?'

She laughed. 'This sounds interesting, and I wish I had the time for the unexpurgated version, but I'm up to my eyes at the moment.'

'Oh, well, it's nothing much. I just wondered if I could bring Grady back — '

'Oh, Patrick! I'm so sorry.' He listened while she explained why it wasn't possible, then offered his congratulations before handing the phone back to Jessie.

'She can't do it?'

'No.'

'I'd heard that reliable dog-sitters are harder to find than good nannies.'

'Possibly, but it's not a question of reliability. Molly is as reliable as they come. It's a question of timing. She's just returned from Downing Street, where the Prime Minister asked her to head a new Royal Commission into youth crime.'

'Oh.' Then, 'She's a High Court

judge?' He nodded. 'She's a bit, well, over-qualified for dog-sitting, isn't she?'

'She's also my aunt.'

'Right. And I suppose if your dog is a delinquent, leaving him with a judge for some corrective training makes sense.'

'Very funny.'

'I'm glad you think so.' She just wished he'd smile again and convince her he meant it. 'What would she have done if you hadn't come home?'

'Managed somehow. If I pressed it, I'm sure she still would, but it would be unfair to ask.' He dragged his hand through his hair. 'Don't worry, I'll think of something. That's your shopping, by the way,' he said, pointing to bags spilling their contents onto the kitchen floor.

'Thanks,' she said, raising her eyebrows slightly at the mess. 'I think. How much do I owe you?'

'I'd forget it if you'd move out,' he offered. One last feeble attempt for sanity.

'Nice try, but it'll take more than a

pound of onions and a bag of chick peas . . . ' She opened the bag. 'What's this?' She took out the toy he'd bought, in a weak moment, for Bertie.

'I wouldn't care to make a guess as to what it is. It's simply a thing with coloured knobs and things to fiddle with. I thought Bertie might like it.'

She stared at him. 'God, but you're an infuriating man, Patrick Dalton.' Infuriating? What was infuriating about buying a child a toy? 'I wish I knew what you're playing at.'

Yeah, well. That made two of them. She'd said it wouldn't work and he was saying, Don't worry, I'll think of something, because maybe, after all, he hoped it would. Even when he had all the evidence he needed to evict her on the spot. 'He's a baby. I bought him a toy. He's the one who gets to play.'

'Why?'

'You ask too many questions, do you know that?' Then he said, 'I bought it because some woman in the supermarket thought I was a deeply caring new man who was shopping for his wife and baby . . . ' He stopped, took a deep breath.

'Patrick — '

'I was probably trying to impress her,' he said dismissively, cutting off that tender 'Patrick . . . ' 'No need to say thank you.'

'This is impossible.' *She was right, he thought. Probably.* 'You're impossible. I've tried, really tried — '

'So have I, but you could try the patience of a saint.'

'How the devil would you know?' she demanded. Without waiting for an answer, she picked up the bag of baby stuff and, with Bertie tucked under her arm, she swept out of the room.

★ ★ ★

Jessie slowed down as she reached the mess in the hall. What on earth had happened to quiet but firm? The moral high-ground? What on earth had happened to two civilised adults sharing a house? What on earth had happened to her?

Patrick Dalton had happened, she thought grimly. One man and his dog. And his dead wife. All tugging at her heart strings. She stepped over the battered plant, the potting compost littering the hall, and went upstairs. Forget sharing. She wouldn't share a house with him if he was Lord Chief Justice.

She turfed Mao out of the cot, replaced the sheets and put Bertie to bed. He grizzled.

The bed had been reduced to a mess of grubby paw prints. She stripped it and remade it. Bertie's grizzling got louder. It was hard to ignore, but she knew he was tired and that he'd probably go to sleep soon. Not that she would leave him until he did. Even if she'd felt like going downstairs.

Patrick had turned the water heater back on, so she decided to take a quick shower and rid herself of the combined delights of baby stickiness and dust from the broom cupboard. When she'd finished, Bertie had stopped complaining.

She smiled as she wrapped a towel round herself. She was beginning to get the hang of this baby thing. If she could just work out how to handle Patrick Dalton her life would be back on course.

She opened the door cautiously, so as not to wake Bertie. She needn't have bothered. Patrick was holding him, walking him back and forth, and Bertie was clinging onto his new toy, biting into it.

'What on earth do you think you're doing?' she demanded.

Patrick turned, regarded her for a moment, then said, 'He was crying.'

'Of course he was crying. Babies do that when you put them to bed,' she hissed angrily. 'If you leave them, they stop.'

'But why leave him to be miserable when I can pick him up and make him happy?'

'I believe it's known as 'making a rod for your own back' in mother-and-baby circles.'

'He's only small, Jess. He's been moved out of his familiar environment. He needs to be held.'

'I'm quoting you theory, not trying to justify it. What, after all, do I know?'

'You're doing fine. Come on, Bertie. It's bedtime.' He crossed to the cot, laid him down. Bertie cooed happily, chewing on his toy.

'I hope you washed that before you gave it to him.'

'Yes, Jessie, I washed it. Now, do you think we could we call a truce? I've organised dinner — '

'No, I've organised dinner,' she said.

'I'll pass on the baked beans, thanks all the same.'

'No, I mean — ' The doorbell rang. Never mind; he could see for himself. 'Will you get that,' she asked, 'while I put some clothes on?'

'Don't bother for me. I like the towel.' His gaze skimmed the point where it dissected her thighs. 'I love the ladybird.'

Jessie blushed and struggled to pull the towel over the tattoo without displaying the rest of her body. 'That is such a personal remark!'

'Yeah?' he said, grinning broadly. 'So, add it to the list of complaints and sue me.'

*　*　*

Patrick didn't wait for the objects to start flying. Really, he couldn't believe he'd said that. But then, if anyone had asked him a week ago, he'd have laughed to scorn any suggestion that he'd be sharing his house with a woman. Particularly one with a baby.

The lingering scent of Bertie's warm little body clung to him. The milky baby breath. He'd missed that. He'd missed it all. First tooth. First step. First word. First day at school.

He dragged his hands over his face. It wasn't Jessie's fault. He mustn't take it out on her. She looked tired. It wasn't surprising; she'd had the kind of day he wouldn't wish on anyone.

He'd had worse, a lot worse, the kind of days he hoped she'd never have to live through, but maybe that was the place to start. They were both having a bad day. Maybe, together, they could do something about that.

He opened the front door. It was the food he'd ordered. A bit early, but perhaps that was just as well. He tipped the delivery boy, took the carrier down into the kitchen and turned on the oven to keep it warm. He had just opened the first carton and was wondering what had gone wrong when the kitchen door opened behind him.

Outside, Grady was poised on the step. He whined softly, his expression deeply sorrowful. Then he caught the scent of chicken and his tail began to wave hopefully.

★ ★ ★

The doorbell was ringing again, and this time it wasn't being answered. Jessie sighed, switched off the hair-dryer and went downstairs.

It was the delivery from the restaurant. She tipped the delivery man and shut the door, then went down into the kitchen. Patrick was nowhere to be seen.

She shrugged, opened the carrier, checked inside the cartons, then frowned. 'Damn!' she said. 'Where's this come from?' Behind her there was a click and she spun round.

Grady was standing on the step, looking mighty pleased with himself. Behind him was Patrick, looking simply bemused.

'You're right, Jessie.'

'Don't sound so surprised. It's not that unusual,' she said, eyeing the dog nervously. 'What about?'

'Come outside and I'll show you.'

It was a trick. He was going to shut her outside with the dog. 'If you lock me out, I swear I'll call the Sunday papers.' She grabbed her mobile to show him that she wasn't kidding. It was flashing 'battery low'. Maybe he hadn't noticed.

'Your battery's low,' he said. 'But you're safe enough. If I locked you out, you'd form a one-woman action group, have a sit-in on the pavement and I'd be left holding the baby. Come on.' He caught Grady's collar and held him to one side as she edged nervously past him. Then he shut the door.

'Now what?'

'Now Grady will show you his new party piece. Open the door, Grady.' The huge dog lifted a paw and pressed it down on the handle. The door swung open. 'Molly said something about teaching old dogs new tricks, but I wasn't paying much attention.' He commanded the dog to sit and then hunkered down so that his face was level with that of the dog. 'Grady, this is Jessie. You make her nervous, so I want you to show her how well you can behave.' Patrick turned to her, held out his hand. 'Come and be properly introduced.'

She took a step back. 'I'll pass, thanks.'

'If you're going to stay here — '

'And I am — '

' — until you can find a place of your own, you're going to have to make friends.'

'Not if you moved out and took him with you.'

'That's not going to happen. Give me your hand.'

'Please don't do this . . . ' she pleaded. He waited. She knew, deep down, that he was right. That the problem was with her, not the dog. Even so, it was a lot to ask.

'Jessie, I won't let anything bad happen. I promise.'

He was so believable. If she'd been on the witness stand, she'd have confessed to bloody murder for a promise like that. Touching Grady was something else. 'I can't.'

'It's time to let the memory of a bad dog fade. Grady will help if you'll let him.' Still she didn't move. 'If Bertie was in danger you'd do it. Wouldn't you? You'd go into the jaws of hell for him.'

'Yes,' she whispered.

'Yes,' he said. 'Well, Grady is nowhere near that bad. He's a thoroughly soppy animal and he wouldn't hurt a fly.'

'Tell that to your plates.'

'Your cat knocked down the plates, climbing the dresser.' His fingers were enticingly close. Long, elegant fingers. Touching them would be as dangerous as touching Grady. 'Your cat bested Grady without raising a sweat. So can you.'

'He's not my cat,' she said as she laid her palm against his, and for a moment he held her hand very lightly, between his.

'We can argue the point later.' She was shaking so much that he wanted to grasp her hand reassuringly, but if he tightened his grip she'd panic and pull away. The chances were she'd do that anyway, which was why he wasn't rushing. He stood up, lifted her hand to his mouth and kissed it. 'Exchanging smells,' he said when, startled, she glanced up to look into his face. 'Now

218

we're one. Let him sniff your fingers,'
he said softly. She made a little anxious
sound deep in her throat. 'I'm holding
your hand. You'll be fine.'

'What if the cat comes by?' She was
clutching at straws.

'If the cat comes by, you'll be the last
thing on Grady's mind. Trust me.' He
wasn't a fool. He knew that this was a
high-risk strategy, but it was obvious
that no one, since she'd been bitten as a
child, had ever made her confront her
fear. He reached out and stroked the
hound's shaggy head, all the time his
thumb gentling her hand. 'Let him sniff
the back of your fingers.' It wasn't so
much that Jessie extended her hand,
more that she didn't snatch it back as
the dog sniffed cautiously, not touching. 'Fine. That's enough. Stay, Grady.'
He turned to Jessie. 'Now you say it.'

'Stay, Grady?'

'Make it an order.' She cleared her
throat and repeated it in a slightly
wobbly voice. Grady did not look
impressed but he didn't push it further.

'Fine. Remember that. Say it if he comes too close, or makes you nervous in any way.'

Patrick went back into the kitchen, followed by Jessie, who shut the door firmly behind her. 'That's it?' she asked, surprised.

'What did you think I was going to do? Put your hand in his mouth?'

'I thought I'd have to stroke him. Or something.'

'First you say, hello. Next time you touch. If you feel like it. It's not compulsory. Now, shall we eat?'

'Oh, yes.' She almost collapsed with relief. 'I was going to tell you . . . ' He hadn't realised just how scared she was. Just what that had cost her and he wanted to hug her for being so brave.

Instead he said, 'Tell me what?'

'I ordered some food from Giovanni's. It's just come. At least something's come — '

'That explains it.'

'What?'

'I ordered Indian vegetarian for eight

o'clock. When Grady opened the door, I was trying to figure out why I'd got Italian chicken at seven-thirty.'

'Oh.' He waited. 'I was going to explain about that. Over a glass of wine.' She looked around — anywhere rather than at him. 'Do you have any plates left in one piece?' It wasn't a serious question, just an effort to delay the inevitable. It didn't work.

'Explain what?' Jessie opened a cupboard, made a performance of searching. 'I've already put some plates in the oven to warm, along with the chicken. Explain what over a glass of wine?' he persisted.

She turned, but didn't quite meet his gaze. 'About saying I was a vegetarian.'

'I'm listening.'

She briefly considered telling him the whole sorry story, right from the time Graeme knocked on her door and sent her life into a tail-spin. But she was tired and hungry and he probably wouldn't be in the slightest bit interested. 'It's a long story.' She finally looked straight at him. 'Can I just say I'm sorry?'

He looked straight back. 'That'll do.' For now. 'Why don't you put the veggie stuff in the fridge for tomorrow, while I open the wine?' As a division of labour it seemed reasonable, if a bit sexist. But she was beyond caring about such things. She even dished up, heaping the game chips on top of the chicken before she collapsed into a chair. 'When did you last get a decent night's sleep?' he asked as he put a glass into her hand. She experienced a memory flash of the moment she'd woken up to find him looking down at her, the overwhelming sensation that she'd just been kissed. Wanting very much to be kissed again.

As if. She hadn't exactly been Sleeping Beauty. 'Sunday night,' she said.

'In that case you'd better take the bed. I'll make do with the sofa tonight.'

'No . . . ' About to be very British about it and say something like, I couldn't . . . really . . .

'Unless you're happy to share again?'

She flushed at the memory. She could take the bed. And she would.

After all, she'd paid a fortune to sleep in that bed — on her own. That was what she wanted, a life without complications. And if he was uncomfortable he might move into a hotel. Then the fact that he'd said 'tonight' filtered through the fuggy pleasure of victory. 'What do you mean, tonight?' If he thought —

'Tomorrow I'll sort out the spare room for you.'

'The spare room? Why do I get the spare room?'

'It would be simpler, don't you think? I'd have to move all my things while you've not unpacked yet. At least I assume that's why you were wearing my bathrobe?'

True. But she wasn't giving in without getting something for herself. 'I take your point. Bertie and I'll take the spare room, but only if I can have sole use of the study — '

'I've been meaning to ask what you do,' he said, reaching for the wine bottle. 'I keep getting distracted.'

She submitted to this minor detour from her point. 'I design websites for the internet.'

'Really?' Why did men always look so bemused when she told them what she did? Anyone would think computers were an exclusively male preserve. 'I thought that was something beardless boys did in their spare time.'

'They do. But they don't make any money out of it,' she said.

'And you do?'

'I'm organised, I'm reliable. I deliver.'

'Not if I don't get the phone fixed.'

She glanced up, not quite trusting this sudden change of heart. Did he think that he could get rid of her by cutting her off from the outside world? 'Don't put yourself out for me, I can just as easily download through my mobile.' Once she'd recharged it.

He shrugged. 'You're welcome to use the study. I have to call in at my chambers tomorrow, anyway.'

'Sole use of the study,' she repeated, 'and a reduction in rent.'

'You haven't paid any rent,' he pointed out, topping up her glass. 'Not to me.'

'That's your problem.'

'I was rather afraid it was.' And he grinned unexpectedly, and all the laughter lines leapt to attention. Grins like that should have a health warning stamped on them, be kept under lock and key where they could do no harm. Grins like that were dangerous. They made you do things that you'd regret when you'd had time to think about it. Because you had all the time in the world. 'Okay,' he said, while she was still trying to recall a bunch of hormones diving headlong into self-destruct. 'But you'll have to spray the plants. What's left of them.'

'You might as well put them in the bin now and save us both time. House plants tend to wilt when I walk by.' She shrugged. 'I was going to order replacements before I left.'

'You're a bit of a walking disaster area, aren't you?'

'Life's too short to waste it pampering boring house plants.'

'I fancy you and Carenza have a lot in common.' She was pretty sure that wasn't a compliment, but she was too busy coming to terms with the realisation that life was too short for wasting, full stop, to retaliate. She was wondering if she should share this sudden revelation when Patrick said, 'This is really good. I'd heard Giovanni's was a great place to eat.'

'It is. I used to go there a lot.'

'With Graeme?'

With Graeme. She nodded and stuck her fork into the chicken. How could she have been taken in by him? Patrick was a stranger — give or take the odd hour in the same bed — and yet he'd been prepared to organise vegetarian food because she'd told him she was a vegetarian. And pay for it himself. 'You'd better make the most of it. I won't be doing this again any time soon, not now I'm saving up for my very own broom cupboard.'

'Maybe you should be putting a little pressure on Bertie's father for financial assistance. For Bertie at least.'

And that was another thing. She didn't like keeping Patrick in the dark about Bertie. But he might just be on a fishing expedition, even now, looking for a way out of the situation Carenza had dumped him in. 'Eat up, Patrick,' she said, ignoring his hook. 'There's zabaglione for pudding.'

'I don't eat pudding.'

'No? Well, then, I'll take mine upstairs, if you don't mind. I need to get in a couple of hours' work before I settle down for the night.' Correction, she needed to put a little distance between her and her disturbing new house mate. She paused in the doorway. 'You don't mind if I leave you to do the washing up?' She didn't wait for an answer. 'Oh, and if you want any bedding, could you collect it soon?'

★ ★ ★

Prickly, Patrick thought, sitting back. She was prickly about being a lone parent, but determined to manage on her own. Maybe he should apply a little pressure himself. Invite a contribution to the house fund from Bertie's father, in order to speed things along a bit. It was amazing what a polite letter from a heavy-weight solicitor could do. And a lot of heavyweight solicitors owed him favours.

Except, of course, he had no idea who Bertie's father was. Apart from the fact that his name was Graeme. And that she didn't want to talk about him.

Maybe he still lived at her previous address. It was on the lease. And if he didn't, he'd surely have left a forwarding address for his mail.

He dumped the pile of pillows on the sofa and considered its merits as a bed: it was larger than average, but not big enough to sleep on in comfort. He'd have to do something about that. Clear out the spare room, buy a proper bed . . .

Which was as good as inviting her to stay for as long as she liked.

And why not?

The idea of it, of having her stay, not just for a few weeks, but permanently, was so tempting that it was frightening.

★ ★ ★

Bertie was sleeping, Patrick was downstairs, presumably stretched out on the sofa. Common sense suggested that it was time to follow their example and catch up on her own rest. Since her usual routine had been suspended for the duration, however, she had to work when she could. Tomorrow she'd take Patrick's advice about sleeping when she could and time her naps to coincide with Bertie's. For now — well, at least it was quiet.

Jessie plugged in her mobile to recharge and set to work. She kept going until her eyes glazed over and then she staggered to bed, checking on Bertie before brushing her teeth, pulling on her nightshirt and falling into blissful oblivion.

* * *

Patrick stirred, woken by the fractious crying of a baby, rolled over and fell onto the floor. He swore, stood up and stretched the kinks out of his back. It was the middle of the night; there was a baby crying. Jessie was right. Memories were more than images on paper. He'd never forget the sound, the urge to comfort.

He paused, unseen, in the bedroom doorway. Jessie had her back to him as she walked the length of the bedroom, rocking Bertie gently as she moved. Her hair was tumbled about her shoulders, gleaming in the light from the hall, her voice sweet as she tried to comfort him. 'Shh, sweetheart. Jessie's here. You don't want to wake Patrick . . . ' She turned and saw him. 'Oh.'

Bertie's voice rose in protest as she stopped moving, stopped rocking him and he held out his arms. 'Shall I take a turn?'

'Oh, but — '

'I won't go back to sleep.'

'I could go downstairs with him. You could stay here.'

He thought about lying down in a bed warm from her body, burying his face in a pillow that still bore the imprint of her head. He wanted more than that. More than a ghostly presence. He wanted the flesh and blood reality. He knew that; he just wasn't sure why. 'You look exhausted, Jessie. Go back to bed.' And he took Bertie from her. Held him against his shoulder. 'We'll be fine.' Then, as she still hesitated, he began to walk in her footsteps. 'Come on, Bertie,' he murmured. 'Your mummy's a busy lady. If she doesn't get a proper night's rest she won't have any energy for house hunting in the morning, will she?'

There was a small noise, small but eloquent. And then he heard her climb into bed and, when he turned, she had the cover pulled over her ears, her back firmly towards him. He smiled into the baby's soft curls, kissed them and then, very quietly, went back downstairs where he stretched out on the sofa with Bertie lying in the crook of his arm.

He was beautiful. Big dark eyes, peachy skin, a smile sweet enough to break his heart. Which was surprising, because he'd believed his heart was already broken, smashed beyond repair.

★   ★   ★

Jessie found them just after dawn, when she woke with a start and raced downstairs in a panic. She came to a halt in the drawing room doorway, her panic seeming utterly foolish in the charm of the scene that confronted her.

Patrick was stretched out on the sofa, Bertie lying against his bare chest. They looked so perfect together, so comfortable. It seemed a pity to disturb either of them. But Bertie must have heard her, had lifted his little head to look at her. She put a finger to her lips, then lifted him carefully so as not to wake Patrick.

He didn't stir, and after a moment she tore herself away from his side and went down to the kitchen.

⋆   ⋆   ⋆

Patrick woke with a start to a sharp sense of loss. He sat up sweating, trembling, and stumbled and into the kitchen.

'Is everything all right?' Jessie turned, startled, a carton of milk in her hand. 'You should have woken me.'

'I didn't want to wake you.' Her expression warned him that he was overreacting, behaving oddly. 'I'm sorry we disturbed you last night.'

He made a dismissive gesture. 'It was nothing.'

'Hardly that. It was kind of you to take him. I should have gone straight to sleep instead of working.'

'You were working?' He was furious

with her, with the man who'd done this to her. 'You shouldn't be working.' Then, dragging his hands through his hair, he said, 'I'm sorry, it's none of my business, but looking after a baby is a full-time job. You need to look after yourself.'

She caught a yawn. 'Maybe you're right. You make a great surrogate father, though.'

His insides contracted painfully. 'Well, you're going to have to manage without me today. I've got a great big hole in my diary that my clerk will be itching to fill.'

'Can I get you some breakfast before you go?'

The temptation to say yes, to sit down and play happy families, was intense. 'No, thanks. I'll pick up something on the way.'

'Right. What about Grady?' She frowned. 'What did you do with him last night?'

'I put his bed in the garage. And I'll take him with me, today.' And with that he disappeared. Jessie shrugged and a while later she heard the front door slam shut.

'And you have a nice day, too,' she muttered.

*   *   *

'Miss Hayes?' The porter at Taplow Towers regarded Patrick thoughtfully and, apparently seeing nothing to disturb him, nodded. 'She left a few days ago. A really nice young lady. I was sorry to see her go.' He shrugged. 'She was a breath of fresh air in this place, I can tell you.'

'Why did she leave?'

'Well, it was the baby, wasn't it? It's in the lease you see, no children, no pets. Are you interested in taking over the tenancy?'

'I'm interested in the baby's father. Where's he?' Patrick extracted a bank note from his wallet and the porter palmed it with a scarcely noticeable movement.

'He and his wife have gone away.' He

shrugged. 'So I heard.' *His wife? Bertie's father was married?* 'It was a bit unexpected. Gave Miss Hayes a very nasty shock.'

8

Jessie dialled up her server to download the work she'd completed the night before, then lingered.

Information. It was all there on the internet, if you knew where to look. All she had to do was type in a few key words and she could find out everything she wanted to know about Patrick Dalton. The cases he'd been involved with. His wife.

She was sharing a house with the man and it would be sensible to find out as much as she could. Apart from anything else, she was responsible for Bertie . . .

Which was about as much piffle as anyone could come up with to excuse a serious bout of curiosity. If Patrick Dalton had meant her any harm, he'd had plenty of opportunity to indulge himself. If she was going to snoop she might as well be honest about her motives.

Except she wasn't quite sure of her motives.

If she'd been attracted to him, looking at him as a prospective lover for instance, well, it would justify her interest. Her mind veered away nervously from the thought. Then inched slowly back to explore the idea, prodding at it cautiously, almost as she would have reached out to touch Grady, uncertain whether it would bite.

'Oh, really!' she exclaimed. So he'd kissed her. He'd probably kissed dozens of women, hysterical or not. All the time. He must have got that good somehow.

And what about the way she'd kissed him?

He'd been upset. It hadn't meant a thing.

Not a thing.

So why could she still taste the salt tears on his skin, the silk of his tongue, feel his arms about her, holding her close, as if he'd truly cared that she was safe, they were both safe?

Her finger hovered over the button for a moment, then she slid the pointer swiftly across the screen. She was working and Patrick Dalton's private life was none of her business.

She'd dispensed with such complications, she reminded herself firmly, turning to check the updates she was working on. Jessie jumped as she saw Patrick, every inch the successful lawyer in his dark grey three-piece suit, watching her from the doorway.

'How long have you been standing there?' she demanded, blushing as she realised how close she'd come to being caught checking up on him.

He pushed himself away from the door, crossed to her desk and leaned over her looking at the web page she'd accessed. 'Perhaps a minute. Maybe more. Are you always that concentrated when you work?'

'Aren't you?' she snapped. 'I thought you were going to your office today.'

'I was, but then I realised I hadn't done anything about the spare room.'

'You're sure you weren't just hoping I'd move on before you needed to?'

'I've bought a bed and I need to clear out the boxes before it arrives,' he said, neither confirming nor denying it. He stood behind her and, taking control of the mouse, began to explore the website she was working on. 'Is this one of yours?'

She turned and looked at the screen, it was certainly easier than looking up at Patrick Dalton as he made himself at home with her computer. 'Yes. This was my first big job. A wild-flower nursery out at Maybridge. Stacey does most of her business on the internet.'

'She exports her plants?'

'No, she believes in native species for native habitats, but she distributes all over the British Isles.'

He clicked onto the 'spring woodland' button, then on a primrose, and was immediately transported to a page detailing the plant, its growing habits, soil preferences, along with delivery dates and cost and an invitation to 'buy me'.

'Very tempting,' he said. 'Do people buy?'

'Stacey's expanding, so I imagine they must.' He continued to explore. 'You could, of course, type in the common or botanical name of the flower you're seeking and get the same result,' she said nervously as he leaned over her, his arm brushing against her shoulder, his breath stirring her hair. She longed to lean back into him, feel his strength holding her.

'And does it pay well?'

'Selling wild-flower plants?' she enquired distractedly, his closeness disturbing her.

'Website design,' he said, and as she glanced up she discovered he was looking not at the screen, but at her.

Jessie felt a powerful urge to reach out to him, to take his face between her hands and kiss him and tell him that she'd do anything, even at the risk of her own heart, if it would make his hurt go away. Instead she said, 'Ask me to design you a site and I'll give you a quotation.'

'In other words, mind my own business?' And he smiled. 'Are you going to be busy all day?'

'Why? Do you want a hand moving the boxes?'

'No. I just thought we might take Bertie out for a walk and have lunch somewhere when I've cleared your room. The furniture isn't arriving until this afternoon.'

'Take Bertie for a walk?'

'It's a lovely day out there. And you do have to eat.'

'Um, yes.' Furniture? She'd thought it was just a bed she was lacking. Recalling her determination to keep it simple, she restricted her comments to his invitation to lunch. 'But lunch out? With a baby?'

'Something simple. Sandwiches in the park, maybe?'

Tempting. Very tempting. But she suspected it was a lot more complicated than he implied. 'I'm afraid it's going to have to be a walk around the garden and a sandwich on the bench, today.'

Treat enough, if it was with Patrick. But she kept that part to herself. 'I'm racing a deadline, here.'

'Work isn't everything, Jessie. And you look as if you could do with some sun.' He straightened and she began to breathe again. 'But the garden will do for now. I'll make the sandwiches.'

He didn't wait for an argument, but took himself off. Concentration, however, was difficult to maintain as he passed back and forth, stripped for action in an old T-shirt and jeans, clearing the spare room of the cartons stored away there. He was taking them downstairs, getting rid of them, and she wondered what they contained. He didn't seem the kind of man who would hoard junk for the sake of it.

'Can I help?'

'No need. It's nearly done.' Then, as if sensing the unasked question, he said, 'I should have shifted this stuff a long time ago.'

'What are you doing with it?'

'Bella used to help out at a women's

refuge. Advice, that kind of thing. I took it on after she died. They'd be glad of . . . ' He stopped for a moment. 'She would want her things to be of use.'

'I'm sure she would.' She looked around, saw the vacuum cleaner. 'Well, I can clean the carpet, anyway.'

'At the rent you're paying?'

'You can always lower it. I'm not proud.'

He grinned. 'Yes, well, maybe I will. We have to talk about that. But normal cleaning services will be resumed on Monday when Mrs Jacobs gets back from her holiday.'

'Mrs Jacobs?'

'She comes in for a couple of hours every morning.'

'Really? Carenza didn't mention her.'

'Carenza probably thought the fairies did it while she slept,' he said, with a wry smile. 'But this room hasn't been touched for a while.'

'Why?' Too late, the word was out before she could recall it and she saw him retreat mentally.

Why? Patrick didn't immediately answer her. How many times had he asked himself that question? Why Bella? Why Mary Louise? Why him? There were no answers.

He stared down into the garden at the tree where he'd planned to hang a swing, to the spot he'd picked out for the sandbox. Well, maybe Bertie would enjoy a sandbox.

He could have told her that it had been his baby daughter's nursery, but instead he reached up and unhooked the faded print curtains that framed the windows before turning to answer her question. 'It wasn't needed.' Then he ran his hand over the wall. 'I should redecorate.'

'If you were thinking of rushing out right now to buy a pot of paint, don't! Please!'

'Let me know if you change your mind.' And he realised he was smiling. 'I'd let you choose the colour. Maybe you'd prefer paper — '

'Patrick! Yellow is fine. It's sunny.

Bright. Perfect.' He held up his hands in mock surrender. 'Yesterday you couldn't wait to get rid of me,' she reminded him. 'What's brought about this change of heart?'

'I'm honouring your lease, Jessie. At least, I'm honouring your new lease.'

'But I don't need — '

'Your new lease,' he persisted, 'which will have the advantage of being legal.'

'Legal? The one I have is one hundred per cent legal. At least . . .' She hesitated, something in his face warning her that she was about to step into quicksand. 'You'd better tell me.'

'Sarah, the girl at the letting agency, was Carenza's old school-friend, Sarah Blakemore. When you phoned up in a desperate state to move into somewhere immediately, the agency couldn't help you. They have this thing about taking up references, which takes a while. So Sarah, eager to help out her old chum, put you in touch with Carenza and even threw in the standard agency lease.'

'The agency didn't know?'

'Hadn't a clue. In fact the manager was rather cross, which was why I had them draw up another agreement and paid their fee, just in case they decided to get nasty. You'll find it on the hall table. You simply need to countersign it.'

'But . . . ' She tried to take it in. 'You could have got rid of me.'

'I suppose I could.'

'What's the catch?' she demanded.

'No catch. No strings. Not all men are . . . well . . . ' His shrug suggested a word he'd rather not use. 'Fill in the space with whatever word you feel most appropriate. You need somewhere to stay. I have more room than I need.' He glanced around at the bare room, his expression unreadable. 'Don't let's get complicated about it.'

'I . . . ' About to ask him what he planned to do with Grady, she changed her mind. He'd gone the full nine yards to accommodate her, to honour an obligation he'd been burdened with by his thoughtless niece. She couldn't ask him to live without his dog. 'Thank you, Patrick.'

'I'll take Bertie down, shall I?' He didn't wait for her answer, but crossed to the study and lifted him out of his little seat. 'Lunch in about fifteen minutes?'

'Um, yes. I suppose so.'

Jessie could do a lot in fifteen minutes. Usually. But once she'd vacuumed the carpet, she couldn't concentrate on the website. Instead, she called her brother. He might, with luck, answer the phone himself.

She sighed as the recorded-message service clicked in. 'Kevin, Faye, should you have woken up and be in the slightest bit interested . . . I've moved out of Taplow Towers.'

Not just body, she realised but soul as well. She'd been angry about that, but now, well, she was ready to admit that it would have been a mistake to stay there. It was too easy to run and hide and lick her wounds. Patrick was right: all men were not like Graeme.

She wasn't letting her brother off that easily, though.

'I'm living in Cotswold Street for the time being,' she said. 'Number twenty-seven. You'll get my bill for removal expenses in the fullness of time.' Then she added, 'Bertie's fine, by the way.' And almost as an afterthought she said, 'But if you've caught up on your sleep maybe you could collect him some time fairly soon? I have a life too, you know. And next time you feel like a break, just ask, hmm? I'll make time, I promise.'

★ ★ ★

'A life? She's got a life?'
  'She certainly sounded different.'
  'She sounded more like her old self.'
  'Pre-Bertie?'
  'Pre-Graeme. God, I'd like to wring that man's neck. But I'll content myself with kissing you. You've been brilliant, Faye. I know how tough this week has been for you.'
  'Oh, not that tough. We haven't spent

this much time in bed since we were on honeymoon.'

'All good things have to come to an end.'

'True, but, since Bertie's in such good hands, I think we can safely leave it for another hour or two.'

* * *

'What are you doing?'

Patrick looked up. 'Feeding Bertie,' he said mildly. 'He was hungry. Pasta with cheese. That's right isn't it?'

'But — ' Then, 'How do you know that?'

'There was a list on the side of the box. You're either very organised or have a terrible memory. Whatever, according to the list if it's Friday, it must be pasta.' He offered Bertie another spoonful. Bertie took it. No spitting, no fuss. Patrick was a lot better at it than she was, Jessie thought, seriously impressed.

'I'll, um, make his bottle, then.'

'It's done,' he said. 'Cooling.'

'You're quite the expert.'

'That's debatable, but I'm quite capable of reading a few simple instructions. So you can stop hovering like a nervous wasp, sit down and help yourself to a sandwich.' He reached over and poured her a glass of wine. 'Since we're picnicking at home, I thought we might as well take advantage of a fridge close by and no by-laws to forbid drinking in a public place.'

'Right,' she said, a little breathlessly. About to join him on the garden bench, she spotted Grady lying beneath the table at his feet. The dog's head was lying flat against the grass and he simply rolled his eyes in her direction, sighed and closed them. Patrick, noting her hesitation, slid along the seat.

'I'll take his head, you can have the tail.'

'Thanks,' she said. 'I think.' And she lowered herself gingerly onto the edge of the seat, picked up her glass and sipped the wine. 'You're a great improvement on Carenza as a landlord.'

'Despite the dog?'

'Dog . . . cat . . . ' She took another sip of wine to take her mind off her twitching ankles. 'Do you want me to take over now?'

'No, we're nearly done.' He caught a dribble of food expertly with the spoon and shovelled it into Bertie's mouth. 'How old is he?'

'Er . . . ' Her hand jerked nervously as Grady's tail flicked against the back of her legs and she slopped wine onto her skirt. Patrick handed her a napkin and she dabbed at the stain, reminding herself quite firmly that tails don't bite. 'Um . . . six months, give or take a few days.' She took a sandwich. 'Golly, this is good. You're incredibly domesticated.'

'For a man? If I'd made that kind of comment about your skill with a computer, you'd have accused me of being patronising.'

'Man, woman, you beat the heck out of me.'

'Yes, well, I've lived on my own for a long time.'

'No family? Brothers? Sisters?' she added quickly, to distract him from thoughts of his poor dead wife.

'A sister, Leonora. Carenza's mother. She's divorced. My mother's semi-retired now and lives in France. My father's dead.'

'Was he a lawyer, too?'

'We all are. My mother, my father when he was alive, Nora, my aunt . . . ' There was a pause and Jessie filled it. His wife. His wife had been a lawyer too. That was how she'd helped out the women in the refuge. With advice. 'And Carenza will no doubt follow in her mother's footsteps and join the family 'trade',' he continued, after a moment. 'If she manages to pull herself together and get some decent grades when she does her resits.' He scraped the bowl with the spoon and fed Bertie the last scrap of his lunch. 'What about you? Where are your parents?'

'Doing a round-the-world trip. Dad sold up his business a few months ago and they went straight from the retirement party to the airport. They should be in China about now.' She started to get up. 'I'd better get Bertie's bottle.'

'Leave it. I'll get it in a minute,' he said, resting his hand lightly on her shoulder, keeping her at his side. His fingers were warm through the light fabric of her shirt, the gesture encompassing, an embrace of the spirit, and she felt an almost irresistible urge to bend her head and rub her cheek against his fingers.

She looked up, startled by the strength of feeling that coursed through her. Frightened by it. The catch of breath, the hot surge of desire. It might be time to rejoin the human race, but she needed time to get used to the idea. Time to regain trust in her instincts. The dangerous thrill of lust at first sight had lost its charm.

'No,' she said, more sharply than she'd intended as she jerked nervously away from his touch. 'You've done enough.' And she put her glass on the table and leapt to her feet, needing to put some distance between them.

Grady responded excitedly, bouncing up, barking, then flinging himself to the ground at Patrick's sharp command as she let out a nervous scream. 'Oh, God,' she said, 'I'm sorry. I didn't mean to do that . . . I promised myself I'd really try . . . You must think I'm so feeble.'

'I don't think you're feeble. I think you've been badly hurt. You've been dumped by a man you trusted, thrown out of your home on a technicality in the lease. You're tired and overworked and on top of that you're making a valiant attempt to conquer your fear of Grady.'

Jessie forgot all about the dog lying at her feet. 'How do you know all that?' she asked.

He shrugged. 'I'd like to pretend that I've got some special insight into what makes people tick. The truth is more prosaic. I went to Taplow Towers this morning and for a small consideration the porter was happy to gossip. He explained everything.'

She stared at him, scarcely able to believe that he was admitting to checking up on her. 'You've been spying on me . . . '

'That wasn't my intention.' He reached for her hand, but she moved it out of his reach. 'Truly, Jessie. I wanted information, that was all. I was hoping to apply some pressure on Bertie's father to help out with the deposit for a decent place of your own. You'd be amazed what a letter from a lawyer can do.'

Jessie was momentarily speechless at such gallantry. Except it wasn't gallantry; he'd just wanted her to move on as quickly as possible. 'Then, I'm sorry you had a wasted morning,' she said crossly.

'It wasn't wasted. I learned a lot.'

'I'll bet. But you needn't have paid for the information. If you'd asked, I'd have told you. You'd have found out soon enough, anyway.' Kevin and Faye had to put in an appearance soon.

He shook his head. 'It doesn't matter, Jessie. You're staying here. You can stay for as long as you want.'

'The lease said three months.'

'In my version there's an option to renew. Just in case you don't find somewhere you want to buy straight away. It isn't that easy.' He kinked a brow, inviting her to join him in a smile. 'Don't tell me you didn't read it thoroughly before you signed it?'

'Not every word,' she admitted. Jessie was puzzled. If the porter had explained everything, why wasn't Patrick furious that she'd lied about being Bertie's mother? 'You aren't angry?'

'Angry? Why on earth would I be angry? You're the one whose been turned out of her home. You're the one who was left holding the baby.'

'I know, but I should have explained. I would have done, but I thought if you knew the truth you'd insist that I leave.'

Patrick's disgust was palpable. 'What do you take me for?' Then he said, 'He really did a number on you, didn't he?'

Jessie's cheeks flamed. He not only knew that she'd lied to him, by omission at any rate, about Bertie. He'd found out all about Graeme, too. God that was so embarrassing. She covered her hot cheeks with her hands and wondered, with an inward groan, just how much he'd found out at her previous address.

She supposed the Towers' porter had given him that, too. Her mail had been redirected from there for weeks. And presumably an open wallet had done the trick there, too, while she'd been too fastidious to use the public information services of the internet to check up on him.

'Excuse me,' she said stiffly, as reality clicked in and she worked out exactly what was going on. 'I'll take Bertie, if you don't mind.'

'Don't be like this.' He stood up, caught her arm and wouldn't be shaken off. 'Please stay and finish your lunch.'

'It would choke me. And I'd prefer it if we revert to Ms Hayes and Mr

Dalton,' she said, staring at his hand until he removed it.

'I really *was* trying to help,' he said.

'Really? You weren't trying to make me feel thoroughly sickened, so that I'd tell you where you could stick your fancy new lease? And its option to renew?'

'Why would I do that?'

'Because then you'd be rid of me and if I complained you could point to the lovely lease I've just signed, you could point out the reduced rent, the newly acquired furniture; I would just be some stupid, hysterical female who didn't know when she was well off!' Then, because she was dangerously close to tears, she turned and stormed towards the house. Grady bounded after her. 'Stay!' she snapped, and he responded instantly. She was still getting over the shock when Patrick called out.

'And will you walk out, Ms Hayes?'

She swung round to face him. 'Not a chance, my Learned Friend,' she replied. 'Not a chance.'

'I just thought I'd ask,' he returned

mildly. 'In case I needed to cancel the bed.'

Jessie glared at him. To her astonishment, Patrick Dalton QC just laughed. Well, she could fix that. 'If you cancel it, Mr Dalton, I guarantee that you'll be sleeping on the sofa for the foreseeable future.'

'Yes, ma'am,' he said. But as she swept through the kitchen, grabbing Bertie's bottle on the way, she fancied that his laughter followed her all the way up the stairs.

★ ★ ★

She was working when the furniture arrived. She determinedly ignored the comings and goings, refusing to look even when she heard a woman's voice, refusing to be impressed, or offer to help. She wouldn't even give Patrick the satisfaction of getting up and shutting the study door to block it all out.

'It's finished, Jessie. Do you want to check it out?'

He'd been standing in the doorway for a least a minute. And he knew she knew he was there. 'I'm sure it'll be fine.'

'Maybe you should check that the mattress is to your liking.'

'If it's not, you can sleep on it.'

'I'll resist the temptation to ask if that was an invitation . . . ' She glared at him. 'I'll just say that it's not too late to change the mattress if you don't find it comfortable. So check it, or live with it.'

She sighed. 'Very well. If you insist.' She swept past him into her new room. And then stopped. It had been transformed. New, mossy green curtains billowed at the window, the bed and dresser were identifiably French-provincial, the linen country-fresh.

The delivery men stood on the landing, awaiting her approval, along with the woman who had apparently organised the linen, hung the curtains and dressed the bed. 'Patrick, I don't know what to say.'

'That means she likes it,' the foreman

said confidently.

'I'd rather hear it from the lady.' He indicated the bed.

She tested the springs. 'It seems fine,' she said.

'You don't think you should lie down and make sure?'

He was teasing now. And maybe she had been a bit harsh in her judgement of him. 'Maybe I should.' She kicked off her shoes, sat on the edge of the bed and then stretched out on it. 'It's wonderful,' she said, linking her hands behind her head on the pillow. 'I'd invite you to try it, but you might want to swop.'

'That good, hmm?' He sat on the other side of the bed, then stretched out beside her and Jessie's traitorous heart picked up a beat. 'You're right.' He grinned up at the delivery man. 'We'll keep it,' he said, and without moving he accepted the clipboard, signed the worksheet and produced a tip from his shirt pocket. 'Shut the door on the way out, will you?'

Neither of them spoke while the workmen departed. A minute or two later the front door banged shut, and gradually the silence crept back until all Jessie could hear was the sound of her own pulse hammering in her ears. Finally, when she couldn't stand it any longer, Jessie said, 'You didn't have to go to all this trouble, Patrick. All I needed was a bed for a few weeks . . . '

'You were going to keep your clothes in a couple of suitcases, I suppose?'

'Well . . . ' glancing at him uncertainly, she conceded ' . . . maybe not.'

He continued to regard the ceiling with the same concentration he'd apply to that of the Sistine Chapel. 'If you're going to stay, you should be comfortable.'

How could she have ever thought Graeme was good-looking? Compared to the man beside her, he was merely pretty. And weak. All surface, no depth. Patrick's profile was spare, strong . . . She clutched at the bedclothes with her hands to stop herself from touching his face, taking the firm curve of his lower lip between hers, tasting it, possessing it . . . 'You'll never get rid of me like this you know,' she said quickly.

'No? Well, maybe I'm getting used to having you around the place.' He turned then, and looked at her. 'Maybe I don't want to get rid of you.'

Her heart, which until then had been loud but steady, appeared to skip a beat. 'I'm not domesticated, you know. I can't cook . . . '

'Not even nut cutlets?' His voice was like silk against her skin. It was time to move.

'Especially n-not n-nut cutlets,' she stammered, fixed to the spot.

'Why not? You like to eat, don't you?' He was so in control, teasing her.

'Of course I do, but for one . . . ' she snatched at a breath ' . . . mostly for one, anyway, there never seemed much point in getting complicated.'

'You ate out? When you were together?' He sounded surprised at that. 'You and Graeme?'

He wanted all the grubby details, then. Disappointed in him, she found it less of a problem to breathe. 'No. We had take-aways, mostly. I was busy, he couldn't . . . or rather wouldn't . . . make the effort.' Why should he? When he'd had her to do it for him?

'My mother always says it's a mistake to trust a man who can't look after himself,' he told her. 'You can never be sure of his motives. Does he want you for yourself? Or just someone who knows how to open a can?'

'My mother always told me you can tell everything you need to know about a man by the way he handles lost luggage, rain on an outing and Christmas tree lights,' she replied. 'Unfortunately lost luggage and Christmas tree lights don't feature frequently enough to be a particularly useful gauge of character. And we didn't do 'outings'.' She turned to him. 'Self-sufficiency is much more telling. Your mother is a wise woman.'

'So she's fond of telling me. Person-ally, I always thought it was an underhand way of getting me to learn to cook and clean up after myself. How did you meet him?'

She was surprised how easy it was to talk about Graeme. How little it hurt, now. 'He knocked on my door. He wanted to borrow a jar of coffee, just like that stupid ad on the television.' It was such a cliché that she should have recognised it for the ploy it was, but she'd been too knocked back by the dazzling smile, the exquisite styling of his floppy fair hair, the Greek-god physique to muster a coherent sentence, let alone a sensible thought. 'Well, he was an actor. At least he claimed to be. Maybe he'd auditioned for the part. Whatever, I fell like a ton of bricks for his helplessness and his killer smile. With the twenty-twenty vision of hindsight, I suspect he practised them both in a mirror.'

'He was a neighbour?' Patrick appeared taken aback by that.

She frowned as she turned to look at him. 'No, he was staying with some friends who shared a flat on the floor above mine. Sleeping on the sofa. Something, again with hindsight, I imagine he did quite often.'

'Oh, I see.'

'Unfortunately, I didn't. I suspect my good neighbours didn't want him cluttering up their living room longer than absolutely necessary and there was me, conveniently unattached and with a comfortable double bed only being half used . . .'

'Nice people.'

'They probably were. Well, not nice, maybe, but a bit desperate to be rid of an unwelcome guest.' She smiled, too, then. 'Rather like you.'

'Ouch.'

'You're right. I'm sorry.' She instinctively put out a hand, clasped his. 'You're not a bit like them,' she said. 'Not a bit.'

'You're too generous for your own good.'

'Yes,' she said, with feeling. 'Being besotted with a man does have that effect. Fifty pounds here, because he had an audition to go to and needed a hair-cut. A hundred pounds there because he had to take his agent out to lunch. It soon mounts up. It was only when my bank statement arrived that the cold light of reason dampened my ardour. This two-can-live-as-cheaply-as-one idea isn't entirely true, you know.'

'I know.'

Damn! She hadn't meant to remind him of his wife. 'Yes, well, the suggestion that he might care to contribute to living expenses dampened his. Ardour, that is. Although he had a nice line in distraction . . . ' How many times had he used the 'this is my mother's engagement ring' routine on women he'd persuaded to keep him? How many times had it been thrown back at him to use again? She should have flung it in the rubbish where it belonged.

'And your neighbours never let on?'

'That it was a regular thing? No. Why should they? They were his friends, not mine. It was why I couldn't stay there, afterwards. When I realised. Bumping into them in the hall . . . I just felt stupid and angry. I needed to get away from that.'

'But I thought you moved because —?' He stopped, shrugged. 'It doesn't matter.'

'You're right, it doesn't. It's over now. Forgotten.'

'You're very . . . accepting. I've known people to commit murder with less provocation.'

'That's because you're a lawyer. You meet people who've reached the end of their tether. I'd simply made a fool of myself. Allowed him to make a fool of me.' She stretched out. 'I admit for a while I was low. I felt used. Sickened. Absolutely determined never to get involved with another man in my entire life.'

'But?' he enquired softly, rolling onto his side, moving closer, still keeping her hand in his.

'But?' she repeated thickly.

'It sounded as if there was a 'but' coming.'

'Did it?' She swallowed. Hard. 'I

suppose there was. This is it, Patrick. Life. It might not be perfect, but there are no dress rehearsals. You have to mop up the messes, put them behind you and move on . . . ' Her voice dried up as he lifted his hand to her cheek, stroked his thumb across her lips, then slid his fingers through her hair before gathering her into him, in a prelude to the kind of kiss that could only have one outcome.

'Stay,' he said. 'I want you to stay.'

Every cell in her body was urging her to commit, to say, Yes. Please. To abandon common sense, and the hard lessons she'd learned, and dive head-long into the shark-infested waters of the mating game. But not like this. She needed to be in control, to make a rational decision, not an emotional one that was based purely on a desperate need to be held, to be loved. Next time she was going to get it right.

'Patrick . . . '

He kissed her, not on the mouth, but on the fore-head, and was off the bed with the width of the room between them before she could protest, before she could regret it.

'Patrick!' He stopped in the doorway as she swung herself off the bed, went to him and put her hand on his arm. 'Thank you. For all this.'

'You're welcome.'

'As for staying — '

'As long as you need,' he said, interrupting her. 'If I can do anything to help with the flat search, with a solicitor, let me know.'

He sounded distant and she let her hand fall. 'It'll take a while to find anything to match this,' she said, turning away abruptly to look down into the garden. Then, still not meeting his gaze, she said, 'I'd better move the cot out of your way so that you can get your own room back to normal.'

Patrick didn't think the room mattered much. It was the person you were sharing it with that made it right. But he had plenty of time. His body might be urging him to make up for the ten years he'd spent wandering in the wilderness, but he needed to reassure her that his heart was along for the ride.

'Leave it,' he said. 'Bertie's still asleep and you've got work to do. So you keep telling me. I'll see to it later.'

9

Jessie went into the study and shut the door behind her. Patrick Dalton was too distracting by half.

But concentration did not come easily. She could hear him moving about above her, in the attic. The shifting of heavy objects. And he made several trips down to the floor she was working on. If he was intent on house-clearing, she wished he'd do it some other time.

She stared at the screen in front of her but it was as if her mind was attuned to him and refused to be distracted by anything as important as work.

Finally the bumping stopped but the quiet was, if anything, worse, and she abandoned the complexities of design and made some phone calls instead. Just to stop herself from going out to

273

see what he was doing. Just to stop herself thinking about him.

*   *   *

Patrick rubbed his chin against his shoulder, trying to analyse the feelings that were flooding through him. Regret. Sorrow for a life never lived.

He touched the gleaming white paintwork of the cot, trying to remember how it had felt when he'd brought Bella and Mary Louise home from the hospital. That bursting-with-pride feeling of invincibility.

The doorbell rang.

If he'd gone with her that day, instead of staying home to work on a new brief, if she'd had Grady with her . . .

The bell rang again and he rubbed the cloth along the rail one last time and let the image go. He could change nothing; all he could do for Bella and Mary Louise was to live his life well. Starting now. Without wasting another moment on regret.

Jessie opened the study door as he passed. 'Oh, I heard the doorbell,' she said, looking slightly flustered, a bit guilty, like a women caught waiting for a secret lover, and he felt a hot charge of jealousy, wanting her to look like that for him. 'I wasn't sure if you had.'

'Are you expecting someone?'

'No . . . I just thought . . . you seemed to be working.'

'No, I'm done. I'll get it. You did say you were busy?'

'Yes . . . It's bound to be for you, anyway.'

Damn. Now she looked like a whipped dog. 'Jessie . . . ' There was a series of short, sharp rings as whoever was at the door demanded instant attention.

'For heaven's sake. I'm coming!' He turned away and took the stairs at reckless speed and flung open the door. 'Yes, what is it?' he demanded.

'Oh.' The man at his door took a step back, startled by his curt response. About thirty, with thick hair that just missed being red, he was tall, athletic and looked vaguely familiar.

'Well?' he asked. 'What do you want?'

'Er, nothing. That is . . . I'm looking for Jessie.'

'Jessie?' The response was so unexpected that he took a step back himself.

His impatient caller seemed to take it as an invitation and stepped up into the hall, looking around as if hoping to catch sight of her. 'She left a message that she'd moved here. We've been away, you see. I'm Bertie's dad?' Then, when he didn't get any response, he continued, 'I suppose Jess is a bit cross with me?'

Patrick was not a violent man. He'd too often dealt with the aftermath of violence, seen the pain, but none of that mattered as he bypassed the proffered hand and instead made a grab for the front of the man's jacket, lifting him off his feet and slamming him bodily against the wall.

'A bit cross?' he bit out. 'You think she might be a bit cross? After what you've done to her? What kind of man are you?' But the question was purely rhetorical, Patrick wasn't interested in excuses. 'I'll tell you what kind. You're a sponger and a cheat and a liar, but if you think you can waltz back into Jessie's life and mess it up again, you're very much mistaken. She's living in my house now and no one . . . no one . . . Do you hear me?' he demanded. His victim responded by nodding rapidly. 'She's living in my house,' Patrick repeated, reinforcing the message, 'and no one is going to take advantage of her kindness, or abuse her love ever again.'

'Excuse me, but I think — '

'I don't want to know what you think. What you think is of no interest to me. I just want you out of Jessie's life — '

'Patrick!' Jessie hurtled downstairs towards them and as he looked up, saw her face, heard the urgency in her voice, his heart sank. 'Let him down! What on earth do you think you're doing?'

He looked at the man he had pinned

to the wall, then he looked at Jessie, her lovely face betraying her concern. She might try to convince herself that she was over Bertie's father — she'd done a pretty good job of convincing him — but one look was enough to show him that this was never going to be over for her. No matter how badly Graeme behaved, all he'd have to do to get a hero's welcome was turn up.

'Making a fool of myself?' he suggested bitterly. Then he released the man and stepped back, colliding with the hall table. He put out his hand to steady it and encountered the lease he'd left there when he'd come home full of . . . life. He picked it up and rent it in two. 'One room, single occupancy,' he said as Jessie's mouth dropped open. 'I don't take couples.'

'What?' Then, 'Are you going mad, or is it me?'

'I once asked you that. Now we know. It's a close-run thing, Jessie, but since you're the one welcoming the prodigal back with open arms, I think you take the honour.'

'Of course I'm welcoming him. I've been ringing him all week. He's come to collect Bertie, Patrick,' she said carefully. 'Come to take him home.' Then, turning to her brother, she asked, 'Isn't Faye with you?'

Kevin cleared his throat. 'She's looking for somewhere to park. And taking her time about it.' He glanced at Patrick. 'We weren't sure what reception we'd get.'

'Oh, come here, idiot!' Jessie flung her arms about him and hugged him. 'Have you had a good rest?'

'I haven't been out of bed for three days.' Then he grinned. 'Whether it was entirely restful . . . ' He leaned closer. 'Who's the gorilla?' he murmured.

'Gorilla?' She was assailed by the image of a gorilla in a barrister's wig and gown and giggled. 'The gorilla is Patrick. Patrick Dalton. I moved in with him when I was kicked out of my flat . . . ' With him? That didn't sound quite right, but explanations could wait.

Then she said, 'Patrick?' He looked white about the mouth and was still staring at Kevin as if he would like to dismantle him with his bare hands. 'Patrick, this is Kevin.' He didn't move. 'My brother, Kevin,' she added carefully.

'Your *brother*?' Now she'd told him, he could see the likeness. But . . . 'But he said he's Bertie's father.'

'Well, yes. The porter told you . . . ' She faltered. 'You said he told you.'

'He told me that you had to leave Taplow Towers when the baby arrived. That the child's father had gone away suddenly, with his wife.'

'Yes. Kevin and Faye . . . ' She glanced at Kevin. 'You'd better go and find her, tell her it's safe to come in.'

'I'm not so sure of that,' he said, keeping a close eye on Patrick.

'Don't be silly. There's been some kind of stupid misunderstanding. We'll sort it out over a cup of tea.'

Kevin waited for Patrick to endorse the idea. Jessie pulled off her spectacles and lifted her eyebrows encouragingly. Patrick threw up his hands. 'By all means, come in. Bring your wife. Invite the family. Make yourself at home. But forget tea. What I need right now is a drink.' He turned as an attractive young woman waved a white hankie from the doorway.

'Is it safe to come in?'

'Faye!' Jessie swooped down on her and hugged her before holding her at arm's length. 'You look wonderful. The rest cure obviously worked.'

'You're not angry?'

'Well, I'd have preferred it if you'd asked first. It would have been so much easier if I'd stayed at your place. You wouldn't have had to ship the nursery by express delivery, and I wouldn't have been thrown out of my home.' Faye didn't quite meet her gaze. Kevin found something of riveting interest at his feet. And suddenly the penny dropped. 'Oh, I see.'

'We had to get you out of there, Jess. All that quiet respectability. You'd have shrivelled up,' Faye said. Then, still not quite sure where to look, she glanced around her. 'This is nice . . . ' Her voice trailed off and Jessie finally took pity on her.

'Yes, it is. The rent's very reasonable too. And the landlord is a whizz at handling babies . . . ' She met Patrick's gaze and didn't like what she saw. 'Come up and see Bertie. Just wait until you see his tooth . . . '

'Jessie?' Patrick's voice, the kind he probably used to question hostile witnesses, cut through the witter. 'Would you mind explaining what the hell is going on?' Patrick made a move towards her, but she took Faye's arm and headed for the stairs, pausing only to pat Kevin on the arm.

'Your cue, big brother. I'll leave you to tell Patrick what you did to me and why. Make it good, because you'd better hope he feels sorry enough for me to stick that lease back together.' And she finally looked straight at Patrick. 'I like it here.'

Kevin looked from her to Patrick and

then, grinning, back again. 'If that's how it is, little sister, I think you should do your own explaining. Just to be on the safe side.'

'I second that,' Faye said, grabbing her husband's hand and hauling him towards the stairs. 'Don't worry about us. We can find the teapot — '

'Forget tea,' Jessie said. 'I'm with Patrick on this one.' She glanced at him and received no encouragement. 'In fact now might be a good time to get out that brandy you seem determined to tip down my throat on every occasion.' She turned in the doorway and looked at Kevin and Faye. 'You'll find Bertie upstairs, in the room on the right — '

'And the kitchen's downstairs,' Patrick added. 'Make yourselves at home.' Then he closed the door and turned to Jessie, leaning back against the door as if to prevent any sudden bid for freedom. Saying nothing.

'Brandy,' Jessie said, after a moment. His voice stopped her as she headed across the room. 'Bertie's not your baby.'

She turned abruptly. 'But I thought — '

'Graeme's not his father.'

'No! Patrick — '

'Then I've got just one question.'

'Only one?'

'What the hell have you been playing at?'

'Playing at?'

'Playing, pretending, call it what you like. Distressed lone mother thrown onto the streets. What was all that about?'

'But you knew Bertie wasn't mine. You said so. You went to Taplow Towers — '

'Where I was told that you'd had to move out because of the baby. That the father had gone away with his wife — '

'You thought I was having an affair with a married man?' Jessie exclaimed. 'How could you?' She didn't wait for an answer but grabbed the decanter and poured out two large measures of brandy, taking a quick gulp from hers. Then choked. He did nothing to help, just waited until she'd regained the use of her lungs. 'Well? Did you?' she finally managed to gasp out.

'If it helps, I never believed for a minute that you knew he was married. Why didn't you tell me Bertie wasn't your baby straight away?'

'I was going to . . . ' She faltered, shrugged, found it easier to look at the spirit in the glass she was holding.

'But?'

'I was going to tell you, that first morning. Explain the situation.'

'So why didn't you?'

'Because you said if it wasn't for Bertie you'd throw me out onto the street there and then.'

'I was concussed, jet-lagged and confronted with an unwanted tenant. You didn't expect me to be reasonable did you?'

'I didn't have any expectations. You *weren't* being reasonable . . . '

Patrick dragged his fingers through his hair, trying to get to grips with this sudden shift. No Bertie. No baby. Just Jessie. 'I didn't mean it. Not literally. For heaven's sake, what kind of monster do you take me for?'

'You were concussed, jet-lagged and your niece had let your house without your permission. I wasn't to know that beneath the tiger there beat the heart of a pussy-cat.'

'You should have told me . . . '

'Well, yes, I know that. And I was going to. Then you went to Taplow Towers. The porter knew the whole truth, everything. You talked to him . . . Good grief, didn't you see that I was surprised you were so calm about it?'

Calm? He hadn't been calm. Not inside. 'I thought you'd been abandoned.'

'No, Bertie was abandoned. On my doorstep. By Kevin and Faye. With a little note saying that they were desperate for sleep.'

'Well, I guess they've caught up now,' he said grimly.

'That wasn't why they did it, Patrick. Don't you see how hard it must have been for Faye? They did it for me.'

'For you?'

'I remember thinking at the time that

if they'd wanted to get me evicted from Taplow Towers they couldn't have done a better job.'

'But why would they want that?'

'I felt safe there. No one in that block would ever knock on my door for a jar of coffee and break my heart.'

'Is that what he did? Break your heart?' There was an intensity about him that kept her at a distance when all she wanted to do was go to him, put her arms about him, reassure him. All she had available to her was total honesty. Laying her heart bare.

'It seemed like it. At the time. Worse, he'd made me lose faith in my own judgement. I stepped off the conveyer belt for a while, forgot that we only get one shot at life, no rehearsals. No pain, no gain. Isn't that what they say?'

He crossed the room in a stride, took the glass from her and took her hands in his. 'Jessie — '

There was a tap on the door and Faye's face appeared around it. 'I'm sorry to interrupt but Bertie wants a

287

drink and there's a huge dog that seems to have some objection to me using the kitchen.'

'Oh, right . . . ' Patrick stepped back from the brink. 'I'll come and shift him.'

Jessie stopped him. 'I'll see to it. You stay and talk to Kevin.'

'Are you sure?'

She smiled up at him. 'If I'm staying, Grady and I will have to get used to one another. Come on, Faye.'

'But, Jessie . . . '

'Grady's soft as butter,' she said, with scarcely a tremor in her voice to betray her.

Her brother made a move to follow them, but Patrick stopped him. 'My sister's terrified of dogs,' Kevin said grimly.

'Yes, I know. But I think she'd prefer not to be. Shall we give her a chance?' From the stairs they watched as she approached Grady, who was guarding the door against Faye.

'Sit, Grady.' The voice was brisk; only someone who knew her well would have heard the uncertainty. Grady gave her the benefit of the doubt, sitting to command, then stretching out across the kitchen floor, resting his great head on his paws. 'Good dog,' she said. Then she bent and laid her palm on his head for just a moment. 'Good dog.'

The two men let out matching breaths of relief, then exchanged a smile. 'Can you stay for supper?' Patrick asked. 'It'll be pot luck, but you're welcome.'

'Thanks. We'd like that.'

★   ★   ★

'I'm sorry, Patrick. I should have told you the truth from the beginning.' They were in the kitchen, putting together supper from a mixture of the Indian food from the night before and Patrick's spiced-beef stir-fry, while Kevin and Faye cooed over their clever infant in the drawing room. 'I just thought that if you knew I only had Bertie for a few days you'd get tough over the lease.' She looked up. 'Which shows just how much I know.'

289

'No, you're right. That was my first thought, my only thought.'

'What changed your mind?'

A kiss. One kiss.

'Can we do anything?' Faye wandered down into the kitchen, followed by Kevin carrying his son. 'What a gorgeous cat.' Mao was sitting on the doorstep, while a cautious Grady was keeping his distance.

'You like cats?' Patrick asked.

'Love them.' She bent to stroke him and Mao accepted this tribute gracefully. 'Unfortunately — '

'Bertie absolutely dotes on him,' Jessie said quickly. And she looked at Patrick. She could almost feel him reading her mind. It was like being touched intimately. Possessed. Known.

'If Bertie dotes on him . . . ' Patrick held her glance, and she knew exactly what he was going to say ' . . . Bertie must have him.'

'Oh, but . . . ' Kevin began to object, as she had known he would. An aversion to cats ran in the family.

Jessie, her gaze still locked with Patrick's, said, 'I insist, Kevin.'

Her brother swallowed hard and took it on the chin. 'Thank you. Just as long as you don't want me to take the dog as well.'

'No.' Jessie was firm about that, too. 'Mao is on a short-term lease, and you'll be relieved to know that his owner will want him back in September. Grady has tenure.' And she handed Kevin a bowl of salad. 'Shall we eat in the garden?'

★   ★   ★

Patrick shut the door on his guests. 'Well. It's just you, me and Grady, now.'

'Two of your unwelcome house guests gone,' Jessie agreed. 'With Bertie back in the arms of his parents and Mao with a new home until Carenza returns, I'd better start house-hunting in earnest to-morrow.' Patrick said nothing. 'At least you can bring his bed in from the garage now the cat's gone.'

'You're still here. I can do without

hysterics in the night.'

She raised her eyebrows. 'Hysterics?'

'You might want a cup of tea . . . or something. You put on a brave show this evening, but in the middle of the night, alone . . . '

'I can handle it. Faye was frightened and I thought, Don't be so silly. Grady won't hurt you. And I knew it was true.'

'If you're sure, then.'

'I am. Goodnight, Patrick.'

★   ★   ★

He felt as if he was adrift on a vast ocean and way out of his depth, sure it was too soon to tell her the way he felt. He knew how he felt, had never been more sure of anything in his life. The first time he'd seen Bella he'd fallen in love with her. Then, he'd had no way of knowing that it would last, that it would grow. This time he could be certain. For a while, it was true, Bertie had confused things, confused him. But Bertie had gone and the feelings remained. It was

Jessie alone who had jump-started his heart, Jessie alone who would make him complete.

But her experience of love at first sight had ended in tears. She needed time and he would give her that. Time and space. He was glad he'd made such an effort with her bedroom. There was nothing temporary about it. It had everything she needed, even —

Oh, God! The cot! If she saw it, she'd know . . . She'd think . . .

He took the stairs three at a time, hoping that she might have decided to put in an hour at her computer. But she was standing beside the white-painted cot, her finger tracing the picture of the teddy bear painted on the footboard.

She looked up, her eyes hollow. 'Where did this come from?'

'The attic. I thought it would be more comfortable than the travelling thing Bertie was using.' Then, because the silence was more difficult than the words. 'It was my daughter's cot.' Still she waited. 'Her name was Mary

Louise. She was with her mother, with Bella, when . . . ' He made a helpless gesture. 'She was five months old.'

'Patrick, I'm so sorry. I didn't know . . . '

'She had an appointment at the clinic, just one of those routine check-ups. Bella couldn't take Grady with her and she said, 'He'll be company for you . . . '.' Jessie made a tiny sound, deep in her throat. 'Someone who saw the accident said at the inquest that Bella wouldn't have been hurt, but she threw herself over the buggy . . . '

'Why didn't you tell me?'

'I couldn't. It was too much pain — ' The words came brokenly as he turned to her and she took him in her arms, held him. 'You see people's faces. The pity. That wish that they were somewhere else . . . That they hadn't asked . . . '

She held him, held him and let it all spill out, and tried not to think about what it meant. The empty room with the pitiful boxes. Tried not to think about him moving his slaughtered baby's things for her. For Bertie. And finally, last of all, she didn't want to think about why he'd brought her cot down from the attic and put it here. She was afraid she knew why. 'Come on, now,' she said. 'Let's get out of here.'

'No, I'll move it — '

'Tomorrow. I'll see to it tomorrow.' She walked with him to his bedroom door. And then, because she couldn't leave him alone with those awful memories, she said, 'I'll stay here with you tonight.'

He looked down at her. 'This is getting to be a habit.'

'Not all habits are bad.'

She thought she caught the ghost of a smile light his eyes. 'No sex, then?'

The temptation was almost more than flesh and blood could stand. 'Just comfort. Can you handle that?'

Patrick held her for a moment. He'd waited ten years for his life to restart. He could wait until Jessie trusted him.

* * *

Patrick couldn't sleep. For a long time Jessie had held him and they'd talked. He'd talked about Bella and Mary Louise, about being alone, and she'd held him close as it had all poured out of him.

She hadn't talked about Graeme, but he'd already had chapter and verse about that from her brother. They'd bonded over a shared desire to throttle the man, but, since it was bound to happen eventually, they had decided to leave it to fate.

Jessie stirred, snuggled closer. She needed comfort too. And a man to trust. He could wait. He'd waited ten years. A week, a month, a year . . . He glanced at her, kissed the tumbled hair. Please, he thought, not a year.

* * *

It was still dark when Jessie woke to find herself being regarded by Patrick.

He was propped up on his elbow and some time during the heat of the night had discarded the T-shirt he'd been wearing, so that she was confronted with those square, girder-like shoulders. She tried not to worry about what other items of clothing he might have deemed unnecessary. As far as she could recall he'd only been wearing the T-shirt and a pair of soft grey boxers when he'd climbed into bed.

'You're wrong, you know.'

'Wrong?' He was still wearing the boxers? No, no . . . 'Wrong about what?'

'You thought I was using you and Bertie as substitutes for Bella and Mary Louise.'

'Patrick, it's all right. I understand — '

He laid a finger on her lips. 'Let me finish. I don't want any more misunderstandings between us.' She stared at him, then slowly nodded. He took his time. 'For a while, I didn't understand. I was afraid I might be doing just that. Filling the gap in my life with a neat little mother and baby package that

297

arrived on my doorstep. Needing me. I was wrong.'

'How can you know, Patrick?'

'The baby went home but you stayed. That's all that mattered.' He stroked the hair back from her face, leaving his hand curved against her cheek. It felt like coming home. And stepping off a cliff. He wanted to kiss her, show her how he knew. It was too soon. It had to be her decision. 'What about Graeme? Any last ghosts you want to show the light of day?'

Jessie's stomach clenched. This roller coaster was going nowhere. For a moment she'd thought that he was going to take her in his arms and make her forget. Instead he was insisting that she remember.

'Not particularly. Compared to what you've been through it was nothing. Certainly not worth wasting breath on.' It was definitely time to move out of Patrick's bed. 'Why did you think I'd want to talk about him again?' she asked, delaying the moment.

'No reason. I've been clearing the decks. Sweeping away the cobwebs. Packing up the past. It felt . . . right. I thought you might like to do the same.'

'It's done. Or do you want my entire life history?'

'Only if you want to tell it. But not right now.' Being trustworthy was putting a strain on his determination to take things at her pace. He needed to put some distance between them. Instead he pushed down the cover and said, 'Unless you'd like to tell me why you've got a tattoo of a ladybird on your right thigh?'

She let out an explosive little puff of outrage. 'What is it about men and tattoos?'

'I don't know, but it sure as hell works. When I walked in and saw you . . . ' He stopped, realising what he'd just said.

'Walked in?' She frowned. 'But you were in here. I walked in here . . . ' And then she knew exactly when he'd first seen the tattoo. 'Damn it, Patrick! I wondered why you weren't wearing a shirt.' She tried to move, but his hand was on her thigh and it seemed too heavy to move. 'I found it in the basket and I knew I was missing something. You walked straight into the bathroom, didn't you? Tossed it in the basket — '

'And fell in lust.'

'Lust!' He stopped the words with his fingers, then bent to kiss away her objection with the lightest of kisses. Gentle, tender, not in the least bit threatening. An invitation, maybe. A promise, even. Oh, hell! She scarcely knew him, but she was responding to his touch like a rocket on bonfire night. She'd lain in his arms for hours, but this was different. 'You've got a neat line in distraction, yourself,' she said shakily.

'If I'd said that I fell in *love*, would you have believed me?'

She frowned, then tenderly brushed the hair back from her face, held it there. 'You're not a liar, like Graeme. Nothing like him in any way.'

'That,' he said, 'is true.' Then, as if giving her breathing space, time to think, he said, 'Are you going to tell me about the ladybird?'

She seized it, eagerly. 'The tattoo was Faye's idea.'

'Really? Have I stumbled across the insignia of some secret feminist society?'

'Not exactly. We were on the university basketball team and Faye thought we needed a gimmick.' She couldn't resist a smile. 'Believe me, no team had a more devoted and enthusiastic group of supporters. I don't think Kevin missed a single match when Faye was playing.'

'You mean when you jumped up in those little skirt things . . . ?' He let slip a startled expletive. 'That is so damned — ' He stopped himself.

'Go on,' she said, grinning. 'You can say it.'

'Sexy.'

'Yes, well, we were nineteen and didn't know any better. But lust isn't enough, Patrick.'

'It's a start.' He leaned across to kiss her and his mouth lingered on hers, making his point. 'If I'd said *love*, you wouldn't have believed me? Would you?'

This time Jessie knew there was no way of avoiding the question. No way she *wanted* to avoid it. 'A week ago, I would have said no without a second thought.'

'And now?'

'Now?' She looked up at him, reached up to touch his cheek, his mouth. 'Now I'd believe you if you said the sky was green and the grass was pink. Kiss me, Patrick.'

His mouth was tender, gentle. She wanted more and her lips parted beneath his, her tongue teasing along his lower lip, sucking on it, as if she was drawing life from him, strength, courage.

'Jessie?' His voice was husky, soft.

'One more time, to be certain.'

This time he took longer, determined to convince her that she was safe in his arms. Much later, he lifted his head and said, 'Well?'

'Ask me again in the morning.'

★ ★ ★

'You are absolutely crazy, you know that, don't you? The sun's barely up and if he's here he'll still be asleep. If she's here you'll probably frighten her to death.'

'I can't help it, Sarah. It's like waiting for the other shoe to drop. Every time I turn around I expect to see Patrick behind me. Or my mother. You didn't have to come back with me.'

'Yes, I did. Suppose he locks you up in the cellar for the rest of the summer? Who would know?'

'Don't be stupid. He wouldn't do that.' Carenza fitted the key to the lock, opened the door and punched in the code for the alarm. 'On second thoughts, maybe you'd better go and wait in the car. Keep the engine running if it appeals to your sense of drama. I won't be long.' She ran lightly up the stairs and tapped on the bedroom door. 'Patrick?'

There was no response and she pushed it open a few inches and peered around the door. It took her a moment to disentangle the figures entwined on the bed but, when she did, she grinned, closed the door very quietly and let herself out of the house.

'Well? What did he say?' Sarah demanded as Carenza eased herself back into the passenger seat.

'Nothing. He was asleep.'

'We've hired a car and driven all the way from France for that?'

'It was worth every penny, believe me. Come on, we'll just make the first ferry back if we push it.'

Epilogue

'He's awful. An absolute nightmare. Whatever is Carenza thinking of?'

'She isn't thinking. She's in love.' Patrick stopped pacing long enough to express his rude opinion on the object of his niece's affection. 'Patrick!'

'Sorry, sweetheart.' He dropped a kiss on his daughter's curly head. Chloe continued to grizzle unappreciatively into his shoulder. 'We've got to do something, Jessie. She can't see it, but the man's a layabout, he's just using her — '

'He's very good-looking.'

'And doesn't he know it? I bet he kisses himself goodnight in the mirror.'

'I doubt he ever has to do that. But being good-looking isn't a sin, Patrick.'

'No, but it isn't just that.' He hesitated. 'He appears to be living off her.'

Jessie, half asleep and inclined to let nature take its course, was suddenly wide awake. 'She told you that?'

'I had a call from her father. She's asked him for money.'

'Her father! That must be a first.'

'Exactly. She didn't ask me because she knew what I'd say.'

'In that case, you're right. We must do something.' Jessie rolled out of bed. 'Here, let me. I think better when I'm on the move.' She took Chloe from Patrick and continued the midnight pacing. 'Poor baby,' she said, soothingly. 'Are those nasty teeth giving you a hard time?'

'Darling, they're giving us all a hard time.'

'Yes,' she said thoughtfully. Then, as she turned, she said, 'Maybe that's the answer.'

'What is?'

'Carenza's boyfriend is just too comfortable. Cosy flat, three meals a day and no pressing need to find a job, with Carenza on tap whenever he feels like — '

'Jessie, please!'

'We need to make him uncomfortable,' she said, glancing up, waiting for her husband to catch on. 'Give him a hard time.' She kissed her precious daughter. It would be hard, desperately hard to let their darling baby out of her sight, even for a few days. But Faye had done it for her.

'You're not suggesting . . . ' Words momentarily failed him. 'You're really not suggesting we leave Chloe on Carenza's doorstep? Are you?' Then when she didn't answer, he said, 'You are. Darling, are you sure? She knows nothing about babies. How will she cope?'

'With difficulty. She certainly won't have any time left to wait on Mr Wonderful. A week with no sleep, no hot meals, no . . . extras?'

'I get the picture. You're sure?'

'Oh, yes, I'm sure. And the sooner the better.'

'Tomorrow?'

'First thing. We'll have to catch her without her clothes on.'

'And where we will go?'

She reached out to touch his cheek.

Kissed him gently. 'Somewhere she can't find us. Somewhere quiet.' And she smiled. 'Somewhere with a big bed.'

Other titles in the
Linford Romance Library:

THE FERRYBOAT

Kate Blackadder

When Judy and Tom Jeffrey are asked by their daughter Holly and her Scottish chef husband Corin if they will join them in buying the Ferryboat Hotel in the West Highlands, they take the plunge and move north. The rundown hotel needs much expensive upgrading, and what with local opposition to some of their plans — and worrying about their younger daughter, left down south with her flighty grandma — Judy begins to wonder if they've made a terrible mistake . . .

MEET ME AT MIDNIGHT

Gael Morrison

Nate Robbins needs the money bequeathed to him by his eccentric uncle — but in order to get it he must remarry before his thirtieth birthday, three weeks away. Deserted by her husband, Samantha Feldon is determined not to marry again unless she's sure the love she finds is true. So when her boss — Nate Robbins — offers her the job of 'wife', she refuses, but agrees to help him find someone suitable. Accompanying him on a Caribbean cruise, Sam finds him the perfect woman — realizing too late she loves Nate herself . . .

LOOKING FOR LAURIE

Beth James

On finding a dead body in her flat, Laurie Kendal fights her instinct to scream, and instead races to the nearest police station. About to embark upon a cycling holiday, DI Tom Jessop attends the scene, only to find . . . nothing! The body has inexplicably disappeared, and so he dismisses Laurie's story as rubbish. But there is something intriguing about Laurie — she is beautifully eccentric, yet vulnerable too, and earnest in her insistence that her story is true. So before starting his holiday, Tom has one more check on her flat . . .

A CHRISTMAS ENGAGEMENT

Jill Barry

Adjusting to life without her late husband, Molly Reid is determined to make the most of a holiday to Madeira. As the dreamlike days of surf and sun pass, a friendship with her tour guide Michael develops and grows, though she wonders whether his attention and care are just part of his job. Back in Wales, meanwhile, Molly's daughter and son-in-law are hatching a surprise family reunion over Christmas — and it looks like the family could be about to gain some new members . . .

LOVE ON HOLD

Dorothy Taylor

Following a broken engagement, Rosa takes up a friend's offer to work on her Anglesey holiday cottage. When she meets her new neighbour, brooding Welsh farmer Gareth, a powerful mutual attraction flares between them, and she agrees to work on his upcoming barn conversion. But the rich, stylish Erin seems to have staked a claim on Gareth — and Rosa's ex-fiancé Nick is harassing her. Can Rosa and Gareth forge a relationship together — or will their pasts catch up with them and ruin everything?